Barrington Corporation News Bulletin

Vol.1 No. 4

April 1999

• The gossip mill is buzzing about former flames Nick Delaney and Rachel Sinclair. The handsome executive has enlisted the help of his pretty employee to give him daddy lessons. After teaching him about the wonders of fatherhood, can Rachel convince Nick that he's ready for the joys of married bliss...?

• Listen up, all you fellow gossips! Sources say that Sam Wainwright's marriage plans are off. But Sam may not be lonely for long—we hear his faithful assistant, Patricia Peel, has been secretly in love with him for months, and now that Sam's single, she plans to seduce him!

• Can you guess who has become the most sought-after bachelor in the office? The answer is Mike the mailman. He is charming, funny and absolutely dreamy. However, ladies, you better act quickly. Seems that Mike has been hanging around Sophia Shepherd a good deal....

Dear Reader,

This April, Silhouette Romance showers you with six spectacular stories from six splendid authors! First, our exciting LOVING THE BOSS miniseries continues as rising star Robin Wells tells the tale of a demure accountant who turns daring to land her boss—and become mommy to *The Executive's Baby*.

Prince Charming's Return signals Myrna Mackenzie's return to Silhouette Romance. In this modern-day fairy-tale romance, wealthy FABULOUS FATHER Gray Alexander discovers he has a son, but the proud mother of his child refuses marriage—unless love enters the equation.... Sandra Steffen's BACHELOR GULCH miniseries is back with *Wes Stryker's Wrangled Wife!* In this spirited story, a pretty stranger just passing through town can't resist a sexy cowboy struggling to raise two orphaned tykes.

Cara Colter revisits the lineup with *Truly Daddy*, an emotional, heartwarming novel about a man who learns what it takes to be a father—and a husband—through the transforming love of a younger woman. When *A Cowboy Comes a Courting* in Christine Scott's contribution to HE'S MY HERO!, the virginal heroine who'd sworn off sexy, stubborn, Stetson-wearing rodeo stars suddenly finds herself falling hopelessly in love. And FAMILY MATTERS showcases Patti Standard's newest novel in which a man with a knack for fixing things sets out to make a struggling single mom and her teenage daughter *His Perfect Family*.

As always, I hope you enjoy this month's offerings, and the wonderful ones still to come!

Happy reading!

Mary-Theresa Hussey

Mary-Theresa Hussey
Senior Editor, Silhouette Romance

Please address questions and book requests to:
Silhouette Reader Service
U.S.: 3010 Walden Ave., P.O. Box 1325, Buffalo, NY 14269
Canadian: P.O. Box 609, Fort Erie, Ont. L2A 5X3

THE EXECUTIVE'S BABY

Robin Wells

Silhouette
R O M A N C E™
Published by Silhouette Books
America's Publisher of Contemporary Romance

To Ken with love—as always, for always.

Special thanks and acknowledgment to Robin Wells
for her contribution to the Loving the Boss miniseries.

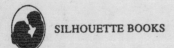 SILHOUETTE BOOKS

ISBN 0-373-19360-2

THE EXECUTIVE'S BABY

Copyright © 1999 by Harlequin Books S.A.

This edition published by arrangement with Harlequin Books S.A.

Printed in U.S.A.

Books by Robin Wells

Silhouette Romance

The Wedding Kiss #1185
Husband and Wife...Again #1214
Have Honeymoon, Need Husband #1238
Plain Jane Gets Her Man #1262
Nine-to-Five Bride #1311
The Executive's Baby #1360

ROBIN WELLS

Before becoming a full-time writer, Robin was a hotel public relations executive whose career ran the gamut from writing and producing award-winning videos to organizing pie-throwing classes taught by circus clowns. At other times in her life she has been a model, a reporter and even a charm school teacher. But her life-long dream was to become an author, a dream no doubt inspired by having parents who were both librarians and who passed on their love of books.

Robin lives just outside of New Orleans with her husband and two young daughters, Taylor and Arden. Although New Orleans is known as America's Most Romantic City, Robin says her personal romantic inspiration is her husband, Ken.

Robin is an active member of the Southern Louisiana chapter of the Romance Writers of America. Her first book won RWA's national 1995 Golden Heart Award.

When she's not writing, Robin enjoys gardening, antiquing, discovering new restaurants and spending time with her family. Robin loves to hear from readers and can be reached at P.O. Box 303, Mandeville, LA 70470-0303.

HOW TO WOO—AND WED—
YOUR HANDSOME BOSS!

By Rachel Sinclair

1) Stay at his house while you help him care for his adorable baby. With any luck, midnight feedings will lead to moonlight embraces.

2) Trade in bland, boring business suits for short, sassy dresses to rekindle the sparks that had once smoldered.

3) Be more outgoing, with everyone except the man of your dreams. Men are always attracted to women who don't seem to want them.

4) Take up an exciting hobby—something he'd never expect you to do. It's guaranteed that he'll see you in a whole new light.

Chapter One

A loud wail cut through Rachel Sinclair's concentration, sweeping aside all thoughts of the profit-and-loss report she was preparing for the monthly meeting of Barrington Corporation's executive committee.

A baby. Someone in the accounting department had a baby.

A feeling of warmth flushed through Rachel's chest. Nothing plucked at her heartstrings like an infant. Hoping to catch a glimpse of this one, she clicked the save command on her computer and turned toward her office door just as her friend Patricia walked through it, carrying a squalling pink bundle.

Rachel eagerly rose from her chair. "I *knew* I heard a baby!"

Patricia grimaced as the red-cheeked, cherub-faced infant grabbed a fistful of her strawberry-blond hair. "You and half of Phoenix. This little gal's got some serious lung power."

Rachel rapidly circled her neat desk. "Oh, she's adorable! Can I hold her?"

"Be my guest. I can't seem to get her to stop crying."

Rachel reached out her arms. The sweet, warm weight of the towheaded child settled into them. The baby stopped in mid-yowl, blinked hard and stared up. Rachel gazed down into a pair of sky-blue eyes fringed with long, wet lashes and felt her heart turn over.

"Hello there, sweetheart," she whispered softly.

The infant blinked again, hiccuped, then stuck her fist in her mouth and leveled a serious gaze at Rachel.

Rachel's chest filled with a strange ache. There was nothing in the world she loved more than babies—and nothing she wanted more than one of her own. Nothing except a husband and a happy marriage. A family of her own was her fondest dream.

The way things were going, though, she thought ruefully, the dream looked likely to remain just that. She was thirty-one years old and her biological clock was ticking like a time bomb, but she still hadn't met anyone she even wanted to date, much less marry. Not recently, anyway. Not in the past two years.

Not since Nick.

A wistful stab of longing shot through her. With practiced determination, Rachel steeled herself against it, mentally cataloguing all the reasons why Nick had been Mr. Wrong.

For starters, he was her complete opposite. She was cautious and careful, while he was a thrill-seeking adventurer. She liked routines and predictability, while Nick thrived on spontaneity and change. She liked gardening and cooking, while his idea of a good time included parachuting out of airplanes and scuba diving in shark-infested waters.

But most importantly, Rachel wanted a home and a family, and Nick had told her from the very beginning that he had no intention of ever settling down.

She should have known better than to ever have gotten involved with him, Rachel thought ruefully, but Nick had been irresistible. Not just because he was handsome, charming, intelligent and funny, although he was all of those things and more, but because of something else—something invisible and electric, something magical that happened whenever they were together.

He freed something inside of her. When she was with Nick, she didn't feel tongue-tied, didn't feel boring, didn't feel caged in by the awful sense of shyness that sometimes made her feel like a lobster trapped in its own shell. When she was with Nick, she felt pretty and fun and witty. She felt attractive…and attracted. So attracted that for the first time in her life, she'd ignored her head and followed her heart.

Well, she'd more than learned her lesson, she thought glumly, gazing down at the baby in her arms. She wanted a man with whom she could build a future, a man who shared her dreams of permanence and stability. The Nick Delaneys of this world weren't cut out to be husbands and fathers, and no amount of wishful thinking would make them change.

Turning her full attention back to the baby, Rachel gently wiped the tears from one of the child's cheeks with her fingertip. The baby gave a tentative grin. Smiling back, Rachel dabbed at the child's other cheek, as well. All four of the baby's teeth gleamed in a full-fledged smile.

"How'd you do that?" Patricia asked.

"Do what?"

"Get her to stop crying and start smiling."

"I don't know. I've just always had a way with babies." She gave the child a little bounce and was rewarded with a delighted coo. The warmth in Rachel's chest expanded. "This one's a real little angel. Whose child is it?"

"Your new boss's."

"You mean Rex has finally hired a new vice president of Corporate Accounting?"

Patricia rolled her eyes. "Yes—finally. After making all

of us in Personnel work like demons ever since Mr. Martin resigned.''

Rachel grinned. The eccentricities of the company's kindly, grandfatherly owner, Rex Barrington II, were widely known by all the Barrington employees. When Rex wanted something, he wanted it yesterday, and he expected all of his employees to pour all of their energies into making sure he got it. His insistence on immediate action occasionally drove everyone who worked for him crazy, but it was also one of the reasons that the company he'd built from scratch was now one of the world's most successful resort and vacation property organizations.

"Rex just wanted to make sure he has the right person handling his company's money, that's all," Rachel said. "Especially since he's getting ready to retire and hand over the reins to his son in a few months." She smiled down at the baby, then looked up at Patricia. "When does the new vice president start?"

"On Monday."

"So soon?"

"Well, you know Rex."

She did indeed. Grinning, Rachel ruffled the baby's blond curls. "Monday is a whole weekend away. What's this guy doing here on a Friday afternoon?"

Patricia shrugged. "Rex insisted he stop by to say hello and meet the rest of the executive committee the moment his plane landed in Phoenix. I was drafted as baby-sitter."

"So who is he? What's he like?" Rachel adjusted the pant leg of the baby's pink playsuit. "He must be adorable if he's this little honey's dad."

"That's what I came to warn you about." Patricia's brow creased into a worried frown. "Remember last month when you told me you'd been in love with the boss you had two years ago…?"

As if she could forget. Her old boss had been none other than Nick Delaney. At the time, Rachel had been an assistant junior accountant and Nick had been the assistant director of the department. He'd been unlike any other accountant she'd ever known, the complete opposite of the usual stereotype. He'd had a way of making numbers come alive, of making accounting seem like a thrilling sport. He'd instigated friendly competitions between hotels, offered monthly incentives to employees with the best new ideas and thrown departmental parties to celebrate both big and small achievements.

He was the most exciting man Rachel had ever met, and she'd fallen head over heels in love with him. She'd foolishly thought he'd felt the same way about her. She'd even thought he'd been about to propose. And then, with no warning and even less of an explanation, he'd abruptly transferred to Barrington's Canadian offices.

The baby suddenly grabbed one of the two tortoiseshell barrettes that held Rachel's curly brown hair away from her face, jerking her thoughts back to the present. Rachel reached up and gently extricated the baby's fingers, giving her friend a grin that she hoped would hide the way the reference to Nick had affected her. "You don't have to worry. I don't fall in love with every man who supervises me. I didn't fall for Mr. Martin, did I?"

Patricia arched an eyebrow. "He was fat, bald and sixty-five years old," she said dryly.

"Well, I don't fall for married men, either. And looking at this little sweetie, it's a sure bet this man is married."

"You don't understand." Patricia's brow knit in a worried frown. "The new director is..."

"Hello, Rachel."

Rachel froze. The voice was familiar—too familiar. It was the rich, husky baritone that haunted her dreams at night, and though she'd rather die than admit it, the voice still flitted through more than a few daytime fantasies.

Her heart in her throat, she slowly turned around. Sure

enough, Nick Delaney stood in the doorway, his dark hair gleaming against the white woodwork.

Her pulse stopped. Her stomach dropped to somewhere in the vicinity of her knees. She clutched the baby more tightly. "Nick," she gasped. "Wh-what are you doing here?"

Patricia stepped forward. "That's what I was about to tell you," Patricia said softly, her voice concerned and apologetic. "Nick is our new vice president of corporate accounting."

Rachel felt as if all the air suddenly had been sucked out of her lungs. She took a step back, her legs as unsteady as her emotions, and was grateful to feel the edge of her desk against the back of her thighs. She lowered herself onto the desktop, settled the baby on her lap and tried to regain her composure. "I—I thought you were in Canada, handling the finances for Barrington's new wilderness destination program."

"I was." He grinned, his teeth flashing white in his tanned face. "But Rex offered me a vice presidency and the opportunity to manage all of the corporation's accounting operations, and it was too good an opportunity to pass up. Besides, Phoenix is a wonderful place to raise a family, and I have more than just myself to think about now."

Rachel glanced down at the infant in her arms. She'd thought she couldn't hurt any more over Nick, thought that her heart had already ached as much as it was capable of aching, but she'd just discovered otherwise.

This was Nick's child—Nick's baby. The baby she'd dreamed of one day having with him.

The baby he'd evidently had with another woman. She swallowed around a hard lump in her throat, her heart breaking anew.

He'd warned her when they'd first started dating that he was a confirmed bachelor, that he didn't believe in happily-ever-afters, that he never intended to settle down. She'd gotten involved with him anyway, secretly hoping that if he fell in love, he'd change his mind.

She should have taken him at his word, she thought bitterly. After all, everyone knew you couldn't change anyone except yourself.

And yet Nick had evidently changed for someone. The thought fired a fresh round of pain through her heart.

Patricia nervously cleared her throat. "I, uh, need to get back to my office. Will you all be all right?"

"Yes, of course." Nick flashed Patricia a grin. "Thanks for watching the baby. You deserve a medal for calming her down."

"Don't thank me. Thank Rachel. She's the one with the magic touch." With a last worried glance in Rachel's direction, Patricia disappeared through the doorway.

Rachel gazed at Nick, her heart pounding rapidly in her chest. He hadn't changed at all. He still had the same jet-black hair, the same olive-green eyes, the same devastating smile, the same ability to make her pulse pound and her stomach quiver.

Tension stretched between them like a taut rubber band. Nick shifted his stance and shoved his hands in his pockets, a gesture Rachel found achingly familiar. "I don't know how you managed to quiet Jenny, but I'm mighty grateful."

Rachel drew a deep, bracing breath and hoped her voice came out steadier than she felt. "Jenny—is that her name?" The child wriggled in her arms and gave another toothsome grin.

Nick nodded. "It's short for Genevieve."

"That's beautiful. *She's* beautiful." Rachel was mortified to hear her voice crack. She cleared her throat and forced a smile. "How old is she?"

"Seven months."

Seven months. Add that to a nine-month pregnancy, and it was clear that Nick had lost no time replacing her in his life.

Another stab of pain pierced her heart, along with a familiar, stifling sense of inadequacy. How could she have deluded herself into thinking a man like Nick would be interested in a woman like her for long? She was as bland as macaroni and cheese, while Nick's tastes ran more to jalapeño salsa.

She should have known it was only a matter of time before Nick grew tired of a boring little homebody like her. After all, Nick was the most exciting man she'd ever met.

Especially when he kissed her.

The thought of Nick's long, slow, spine-tingling kisses sent a rush of heat coursing through her. Nick's kisses had made her knees melt and her head spin and her whole world tilt off its axis. When Nick had kissed her, he'd made her feel like he found *her* exciting, too.

The baby shifted in her arms, pulling her thoughts back to the present. She was embarrassed to realize that her gaze was locked on Nick's lips.

Even more disconcerting was the intent way Nick was looking back at her, as if his eyes could drink her in. She'd forgotten the way he focused his attention, forgotten the knack he had for making her feel as if she were the most important person in his world.

"It's good to see you, Rachel," he murmured. "You look wonderful. Just the way I remember you."

"You haven't changed much, either," she managed.

He drew back his navy sports coat and cast a rueful glance down at large stain on his white oxford shirt. Nick had always been meticulous about his clothing, Rachel recalled. He'd said it was the result of having to wear dirty clothes to school as a boy after doing the morning chores on his family's farm.

He pointed to the yellowed splotch. "I'm afraid I'm a little worse for the wear. The plane trip was a nightmare. Jenny poured a whole bottle of juice all over me at takeoff, then cried nonstop throughout the entire flight. In fact, this is the first time she's stopped crying all day."

Rachel looked down at the child. Her white-blond head was snuggled against Rachel's tan blouse, her eyes half-closed. She looked as if she might fall asleep at any moment. "The poor sweetie. She's probably exhausted."

"Well, she's not alone." Nick ran a hand down his face and blew out a tired breath. "I tried everything I could think of to get her to stop wailing—singing, making funny faces, rocking her, feeding her, reading to her. Nothing worked. I thought the other passengers were going to throw us both out the emergency exit."

"Where's Jenny's mother?" *Oh, dear, why had she asked that?* If she were here in the building, Nick might think she wanted to be introduced. Rachel didn't think she could handle the social civilities of meeting Nick's wife without bursting into tears. She was close to crying as it was.

"She's…" Nick hesitated, his mouth stretching into a somber line, his eyes clouding. "She's dead."

Rachel was immediately ashamed of her thoughts. Her heart flooding with sympathy, she drew the drowsy child tighter against her chest. "Oh, how terrible. Poor Jenny." Rachel gently stroked the child's back. "I'm so sorry. It must have been awful, losing your wife."

Nick's eyebrows flew up. "I didn't lose a wife. I lost a brother. He and my sister-in-law died in a car crash in Oklahoma three weeks ago. I was their only living relative, so now I'm their child's guardian."

The baby wasn't Nick's. An unbidden sense of relief swept through Rachel. Confused by the intensity of her reaction, she kept her eyes carefully focused on Jenny.

"Patricia didn't tell you?"

Rachel shook her head. "She was just getting around to telling me you were going to be my new boss, when you walked in."

"I'm surprised you'd assume I'd gotten married. You know I'm not the marrying type." He gave a crooked smile, the kind that could charm a snake out of a tree. "If I were, I would have tried to marry you."

His tone was light, but the words fell heavily on her heart. He'd always been good at turning on the charm, at smoothing over awkward situations. That was no doubt what he was doing now.

Rachel swallowed around the lump that had formed in her throat. "I—I'm very sorry about your brother and sister-in-law. What an awful tragedy."

Nick nodded soberly. "Especially for Jenny. To make matters worse, she can't seem to stand me." He gazed at the baby and sighed deeply. "Not that I blame her. I don't know the first thing about babies. She must know she's in the hands of a rank amateur."

Rachel softly touched Jenny's cheek, her heart aching for the motherless child. "She's probably just missing her parents."

"I'm sure that's part of it. But Jenny's always been finicky about people. Aside from her parents, the only person she's ever tolerated is an older woman, Mrs. Olsen, who used to occasionally baby-sit for her back in Oklahoma. Mrs. Olsen kept Jenny for me while I settled the details of my brother's estate there. I tried to get her to move here to take care of Jenny for me, but she has a husband and a home, and she couldn't relocate." Nick blew out a long breath. "This is the first day I've been all alone with Jenny, and to tell you the truth, I'm at my wits' end."

"Give it some time," Rachel said. "In a few days, you and Jenny will be thicker than thieves." She glanced up curiously. "What are you going to do with her while you work?"

"I plan to hire a daytime nanny. I've got the name of a good agency." Nick gave a warm smile, the kind that always turned Rachel's insides to melted butter. "I just hope

I can find someone she likes as much as she likes you. It's amazing how well you calmed her down.''

Rachel sifted her fingers through the baby's blond curls. ''I love children. Maybe she just senses that.''

''Maybe so. I remember that about you.'' His gaze lingered on her face. ''I remember a lot about you.''

Rachel's pulse lurched, then pounded madly. She remembered a lot about him, too—including some things she wished she couldn't recall in such vivid detail. Things like the hungry, smoky look he got in his eyes when he was about to kiss her, and the way his eyes closed when his lips touched hers, and the delicious roughness of his clean-shaven chin.

Her mouth went dry. She knew she should pull her eyes away, but she couldn't seem to do so.

Remember the rest of it, she ordered herself. *Remember how he left without any warning. Remember how you felt when you found out that he'd been transferred at his own request.*

Swallowing hard, Rachel turned her gaze to the baby, who was now asleep in her arms.

The air between them grew thick and charged with emotion. Nick uneasily cleared his throat. ''I, uh, hope you won't mind working with me again.''

''Mind?'' She willed her mouth into a smile, hoping it looked a lot more genuine than it felt. She'd be darned if she'd let him know how badly his abrupt disappearance had hurt her two years ago, or how unsettling his sudden reappearance was now. ''Why should I mind?''

Nick shoved his hands in the pockets of his gray slacks and shrugged. ''I was just afraid that, well, since we dated and all...''

''That was all a long time ago,'' Rachel said rapidly, forcing a note of nonchalance into her voice. ''Don't worry about it. It was just one of those things.''

His eyes darkened and a nerve flexed in his jaw. He

opened his mouth as if he were about to say something, then abruptly closed it. "Right." He shifted his stance and pulled his hands from his pockets. "I'm, uh, glad you feel that way."

But he wasn't glad. Not a bit. It bothered the heck out of him to hear her dismiss their relationship so lightly.

Just one of those things. It hadn't been like that at all. When he'd been with Rachel, he'd felt more alive than he'd ever felt in his life. It was almost as if she threw some sort of magic spell over him.

He could almost feel himself slipping under it now. Everything about her was just as he remembered—her creamy skin, her deep blue eyes, her shoulder-length brown curls defiantly trying to escape from her neat, pulled-back hairstyle. He'd always loved Rachel's hair, had always thought that it perfectly captured her personality—prim and restrained on the surface, wild and abandoned underneath, involved in a continual, silent, unconscious struggle to break free.

She looked wonderful, standing there in that tailored navy suit. He'd thought he was finally over her, but all sorts of old feelings were floating to the surface as he stood there looking at her.

He abruptly realized that he was staring. He glanced away, but not before he saw a faint blush stain her cheeks.

"Well, I'd better get back to work," she said. "I still need to double check the numbers on the monthly profit and loss report before I print it out, and I want to get out of here at a decent hour."

"Do you have plans for the evening?" The question slipped out before he could stop it.

Her eyes grew wary. "As a matter of fact, I do."

"A date?" Good grief. What was the matter with him? He had no right to ask such personal questions, but he couldn't seem to help himself.

Rachel looked away. "Not exactly. I'm planning to go to the movies with Patricia and some other friends."

Relief eased the constriction in Nick's chest. He knew that it was illogical, knew he had no rights where Rachel was concerned, but he hated the idea of her seeing another man. "Sounds nice. Anyone I know?"

"I think they all came to work here after you left. You've met Patricia. There are six of us who meet every day for coffee breaks and lunch, and sometimes we pal around together on weekends."

"Are they all women?"

Rachel shot him a curious gaze. "As it so happens, they are." She rose from her perch on the corner of the desk. "Well, I'd better give Jenny back to you." She stepped forward and started to place the child into his arms. Her hands brushed his, and a current of electricity passed between them. He knew she felt it, too, because she froze, her blue eyes wide and alarmed.

Two years had gone by since the last time they'd touched, but time had done nothing to diminish the chemistry between them. It still sizzled, still felt strong and urgent and compelling. They'd always been more than physically compatible, Nick thought; they'd been physically combustible. The problem was, the emotional connection between them had been just as strong as the physical attraction. Things had been getting too serious.

Which was why he'd left. Rachel needed a husband and a family, and he had no intention of ever settling down. Marriage meant being tied down, and being tied down meant monotony, boredom and drudgery. He'd had enough of that to last a lifetime, growing up on a family farm. Besides, his parents' grim, loveless marriage had been more than enough to convince him to remain single. He wanted to see the world, to pursue new challenges, to follow his own whims without having to answer to anyone.

For some reason, though, he had a hard time remembering that whenever he was around Rachel. The memory of how she'd felt in his arms sent a ripple of arousal racing through him. He quickly tried to batten it down.

Getting involved with Rachel had been a mistake before, and it would be a mistake again. He had no right to start something he had no intention of seeing through to an honorable conclusion. He knew how she felt about marriage and family, knew that she wasn't a person to take romantic involvement lightly. He'd known two years ago that she was getting far too serious about him. He'd seen it in the way she looked at him, in the way her eyes lit up whenever he walked into a room.

He'd seen it, and yet he'd postponed breaking things off, he thought guiltily. The truth was, he'd loved having Rachel look at him that way.

But he wasn't entitled to it. The man Rachel looked at like that should offer her forever, and he was not a forever kind of guy.

"Well, here you go," Rachel said, lowering the sleeping baby into his arms. The child stirred, stretched, then opened her eyes. The moment the infant caught sight of Nick's face, her forehead scrunched into an angry frown, her face grew red and her rosebud mouth puckered into an ear-splitting cry.

Oh, no. Here we go again. Nick hated feeling out of control, and he'd never felt less in control in his life than he did with Jenny.

The baby squirmed into an upright position and yelled directly in his ear. Momentarily deafened, he winced and gave her an awkward pat. "Hey, there, kiddo. Everything's going to be okay."

But Jenny wasn't so easily convinced. Her tiny white sneakers delivered a one-two punch to his stomach as her miniature fists flailed wildly at his chest. He turned to Rachel, his spirits sinking.

"See what I mean? She can't stand me."

"She just needs some time to get used to you," Rachel consoled. "I'm sure everything will be fine after a period of adjustment."

The baby struggled angrily against him. "So what am I supposed to do in the meantime? She won't eat, she won't sleep and she refuses to let me comfort her. I'm afraid she's going to make herself sick."

The baby turned toward Rachel, stretched out her arms and screamed at a decibel level that could shatter glass.

"She does seem awfully upset." Rachel's eyes darkened with concern. "Would you mind if I hold her again?"

"Be my guest." He passed the baby back to Rachel. The moment the child settled in her arms, she stopped bawling and gave Rachel a big, gummy grin.

Nick scratched his head. "How did you do that?"

Rachel gave a modest shrug. "Maybe I remind her of her mom."

"You don't look anything like her."

"Babies recognize more than just a person's looks. Maybe I feel like her. Or smell like her."

Nick remembered all too well how Rachel felt—soft and warm and delicious. He remembered how she smelled, too. In fact, from where he was standing, he could catch a faint hint of her perfume—a flowery, powdery-soft scent that made him think of fresh air and a summer garden.

He'd once asked a woman in Canada to dinner just because she'd smelled like Rachel. Both the evening and the woman had been a major disappointment.

"Where are you and Jenny staying tonight?"

Rachel's question jerked Nick back to the moment. "In our new home. Rex hired a relocation specialist to lease and furnish a house for us. The place is supposed to be stocked with food and linens and baby supplies, and one of the bedrooms is set up like a nursery."

"Wow! You vice presidents really get some nice perks."

Nick gave a wry grin. "It's costing Rex less than the

moving service he usually provides for transferring employees."

"You didn't have any movers?"

Nick shook his head. "I don't have enough stuff to warrant it. I had a few boxes shipped, and that took care of it."

He hadn't had many belongings when he'd lived in Phoenix before, either, Rachel remembered. He hadn't wanted to own appliances or furniture or anything else that smacked of permanence. He might have a baby to raise now, but he basically hadn't changed.

Rachel swallowed hard and forced a smile. "It sounds like the ideal setup for you."

"Yeah. It's only lacking one thing. A person Jenny will tolerate." Nick's green eyes locked on hers. He hesitated, and Rachel saw him swallow. "I know you've got plans for tonight, Rachel, and I really hate to ask you this…"

She saw the question in his eyes and knew what was coming. She tried to steel herself against him. She was a fool to even consider it. It was bad enough that Nick was back in town and that she was going to have to work with him. She had no business, absolutely none, seeing him outside the office for any reason.

"I really need some help." His eyes were pleading. "You saw how upset she gets with me. Is there any way you could help me feed Jenny and put her to bed for the night? I'm afraid she's going to get ill if she continues on this way."

Rachel gazed down at the baby. The child's tiny pink mouth curved into a gap-toothed grin, making her chubby cheeks puff out like a chipmunk's.

Rachel sighed, knowing it was a lost cause. She wasn't the kind of person who could walk away and leave a baby in misery, and Nick knew it as well as she did.

She reluctantly looked up and slowly nodded her head. "Okay. But just for tonight. And only because of Jenny."

She didn't want him to think she was doing it for his sake. She had no intention of getting involved with him again on any kind of personal level. In fact, if she were wise, she'd give serious consideration to finding another job.

The corners of Nick's eyes creased in a devastating fashion as he flashed a heart-stopping smile. "Thanks a million. You're the best, Rachel."

The way he said her name sent goose bumps chasing up her arm. She looked away, hating the effect he had on her, wishing she could will it away. "I still have to check over that report before I leave."

"I'll check it for you. You just keep Jenny happy."

An unsettled feeling swept through Rachel as he circled her desk and seated himself behind her computer. He'd been back in her life less than fifteen minutes and he was already rearranging her life.

Well, she wouldn't let it become a habit, she told herself resolutely. She was only helping him out this once. She'd get the baby settled for the night, and that would be the end of any personal involvement with Nick Delaney.

Chapter Two

Twilight hovered over Phoenix, tinting the sky a deep, dusky purple as Nick braked the company-leased black Acura in the driveway of an imposing two-story stucco house. This was it—his new home. He recognized it from a photo the relocation specialist had sent him.

Not bad, he thought, leaning forward to peer out the windshield. Even nicer than the picture had indicated. Located in an exclusive Scottsdale neighborhood, the tall, white house was topped with a red tile roof and surrounded by the kind of lavish landscaping that spoke of professional lawn maintenance. Olive and citrus trees mingled with tall palms and native shrubbery in lush, well-watered abundance.

But of far more interest to Nick than the house was the woman in the blue Toyota pulling into the driveway behind him. Walking into Rachel's office and seeing her again had made him feel as if he'd just taken a hard punch in the gut. How could he have forgotten how she always affected him?

Probably because he'd put so much effort into trying to

convince himself he was over her, mocked a silent voice in his head.

The thought irritated him. He *was* over her. He'd moved away and hadn't had any contact with her in two years.

Oh, yeah? So why had he jumped at the opportunity to come back to Phoenix? the niggling voice silently taunted.

Nick raked a hand through his hair in frustration, drumming the fingers of his other hand on the steering wheel. Rachel had had nothing to do with his decision to move back here, he silently asserted. He'd been working toward this promotion for years. Besides, Phoenix was a great place to raise a child, and now that he had the responsibility of Jenny, that was certainly a consideration.

The thought of Jenny caused an odd tightening sensation in his chest. He wasn't afraid to kayak a raging river, jump out of an airplane at ten thousand feet or climb a bald-faced cliff, but he was terrified of his seventeen-pound niece.

What he knew about kids would fit on the nose of a gnat. He hadn't been around any since he was one himself, and judging from the way Jenny reacted to him, he obviously didn't have much of a natural knack for dealing with them.

It was a good thing Rachel had agreed to help him out tonight. He'd hated having to ask her for a favor, but he'd been at the end of his rope.

He glanced at her in the rearview mirror, guilt tightening his stomach. He had no right asking her for favors—not after the abrupt way he'd left. He owed her an apology and an explanation. He'd give her both before the evening was over, he promised himself, climbing out of his car and striding to Rachel's Toyota.

She lowered the automatic window as he walked toward her. Bending down, he leaned through it. Her navy skirt had ridden up her thighs, and the sight of her slender legs against the blue upholstery of the car seat made his mouth go dry. He'd always loved Rachel's legs. Long and supple and tanned, they'd played a key role in many an erotic fantasy.

Well, he darn sure couldn't afford to fantasize now. With an effort he pulled his gaze away. "How did Jenny weather the ride?"

"She was a perfect passenger."

Nick peered into the back seat and saw that the baby was sound asleep in the car seat he'd strapped into Rachel's car at the corporate office.

"She dozed off before we even left the parking lot," Rachel reported.

Nick shook his head in amazement. "She's an entirely different kid when she's with you."

"Well, most babies fall asleep when they ride in a car."

"Couldn't prove it by me. Jenny cried for two straight hours on the trip from Lawton to the Oklahoma City airport this morning, then screamed like a banshee on the ride from the Phoenix airport to the office."

Rachel gave him a sympathetic smile. Once again, Nick found his gaze riveted on her eyes. He'd always loved her eyes, had always thought they looked as inviting as a feather bed on a snowy day—a warm, soft, comforting place he could fall into and never leave.

Which was exactly why he had left.

Jerking his gaze away, Nick straightened and turned to the house. "So what do you think of this place?"

"It's gorgeous. I can't wait to see the inside."

Nick glanced in the back seat. "I guess that means we need to take Jenny out of her car seat, huh? Any chance we can do it without waking her up?"

"Oh, we need to wake her. You said she hasn't eaten all day. If she doesn't get something in her tummy, she probably won't sleep through the night." Rachel lifted the diaper bag from the passenger seat and smiled reassuringly. "But don't worry. After a nice meal and a warm bath, she's sure to doze right back off."

"I can't tell you how much I hope you're right."

Rachel's eyes grew teasing. "She really traumatized you, didn't she?"

"Completely."

Rachel's smile widened, and he was momentarily dumbstruck by the way it changed her face. He'd forgotten about the little dimple on her right cheek, forgotten the way a smile made her whole face shine and blossom.

He opened her door, then reached out his hand to help Rachel out of the car. She hesitated, then took it. A current of energy raced through him as her fingers curled around his. He'd always felt sparks whenever they touched, always felt a surge of heat whenever she'd entered the room.

Making a mental note to guard against future physical contact, he released her hand as soon as she was on her feet, took the pink diaper bag from her and opened the back door.

Rachel promptly leaned in and bent over the car seat. "Hello there, sweetie," she murmured to the baby. "Welcome to your new home."

Jenny opened her eyes, then rubbed them sleepily. Rachel unfastened the child's safety strap and lifted her out. The baby snuggled cozily against her shoulder as Nick closed the door.

Rachel glanced at him. "She seems pretty docile right now. Do you want to try holding her?"

He'd prefer walking barefoot over burning coals, but he couldn't very well admit that to Rachel. "I don't want to upset her again," he hedged.

"Now that she's calmed down, I'll bet you two will get along fine. She's been around you all day, so she's probably used to you by now."

Jenny was used to him, all right—used to screaming in his ear and flailing at him like a prizefighter. But Rachel was looking at him expectantly, and he didn't want her to think he was baby-whipped. "Okay," he reluctantly agreed, hoisting the diaper bag to his shoulder. "I'll give it a try."

Nick reached out his arms, and Rachel transferred the child into them. The infant instantaneously kicked him in the gut and yelped like a howler monkey.

"I don't think she's ready to be friends." Nick rapidly passed the screaming infant back to Rachel.

The baby quieted with annoying speed. Not that he could blame her, Nick thought wryly, rubbing the spot on his belly where Jenny had scored a direct hit. He remembered all too well how it felt to be wrapped in Rachel's arms—to feel her silky hair against his cheek, her soft breasts against his chest, her heart pounding next to his.

Good grief, he had to get his thoughts under control. Jerking his gaze away from Rachel, Nick abruptly gestured to the house. "Let's go inside."

He strode to the front door, pulled out a key and unlocked the double oak doors that formed the impressive entrance. Carrying the now-smiling baby, Rachel walked inside as Nick flicked the light switch by the door.

The flagstone floor in the foyer, as well as the walls, were the color of sun-bleached sand. So was the thick carpeting in the living room and the upholstery on the elegant high-backed chairs in the adjacent dining room. The entire house, it seemed, was decorated in soothing shades of cream and beige and tan, and filled with beautiful Southwestern-style furnishings.

"It's lovely," Rachel murmured.

"Yeah, it's not bad," Nick agreed.

They wandered through the first floor, past a study with an oak desk and a computer, through a cozy den and into a breakfast nook overlooking the lush back lawn. They ended up in a large kitchen with pickled wood cabinetry and a white granite countertop.

Nick opened the door to a cupboard and was glad to see

that the relocation specialist had stocked it as requested. Rows of baby juice, baby food and cereal lined the shelves.

"How do you know what to feed her?" Rachel asked.

"Her pediatrician in Oklahoma sent a list. I'm supposed to introduce a new food every week." He leaned toward the baby and grinned. "Hey, kiddo, look at this. Looks like we've got the entire contents of the local grocery store's baby food aisle in here just for you."

Jenny whimpered and hid her face against Rachel's neck. Holy cow, you'd think he had horns and six eyes, he thought with dismay.

"Was it something I said? Do I need a breath mint?" He pulled back his jacket and pretended to check his underarms. "Maybe my twenty-four-hour deodorant has expired."

Jenny refused to look at him, but at least he made Rachel laugh.

"Don't take it personally," she told him, patting the baby's back. "Jenny's tired and hungry and probably wet. Why don't we find the nursery and change her diaper? Then we can feed her, give her a bath and put her to bed."

Each task sounded like a daunting undertaking. "Boy, am I ever glad you're here. Where did you learn so much about babies?"

Rachel started walking toward the staircase. "I took some courses in early-childhood education when I was in college."

Adjusting the diaper bag on his shoulder, Nick looked at her curiously. "That's an odd thing to combine with a major in accounting."

"Actually, it started out the other way around. I planned to major in early-childhood education. I'd always dreamed of owning and operating a preschool, but my parents talked me out of it."

He'd never known that about her. "Why?"

Rachel shrugged. "They thought it was too risky. They

showed me a bunch of statistics about the number of small businesses that fail every year, and pretty much convinced me I'd be destined for a life of insecurity and poverty. My folks have always been big proponents of security.''

Nick remembered her telling him as much. "They're both accountants, aren't they?"

Rachel nodded. "I'm a chip off both old blocks." She gazed at him wistfully. "You're lucky your parents didn't want you to follow in their footsteps.''

Nick gave a tight, humorless laugh. "Oh, but they did.''

Rachel's brows raised in surprise. "I never knew that.'' There was a lot about Nick that she didn't know, she mused. She knew almost nothing about his childhood or his family, aside from the fact he was raised on a farm in southeastern Oklahoma. He always changed the subject when the topic came up.

He did so now. "Surely you didn't learn everything you know about babies from books.''

"I did a lot of baby-sitting when I was a teenager.''

"You did? I'm surprised.''

"Why?''

His eyes surveyed her with frankly masculine appreciation. "I can't imagine that you had very many dateless Saturday nights.''

As ridiculous as she knew it was, the flirtatious remark gave her a rush of pleasure. Rachel shifted the baby to her hip and started up the thickly carpeted staircase. "Oh, I was a real wallflower in high school.''

"That's hard to imagine.''

Rachel grinned ruefully. Nick was probably the only man in the world who hadn't noticed she was *still* a wallflower—just a few shades shy of being completely invisible. In fact, Rachel had always thought that her most outstanding attribute was her ability to blend in. Everything about her was average—her height, her build, her shade of brown hair, her features. She could easily be the poster child for humdrum.

The funny thing was, when she was with Nick, she didn't feel average or humdrum at all. She felt alive and attractive and special. And interesting. Exciting, even.

That alone should have told her that their relationship had no future, she thought wryly. It clearly hadn't been based on reality.

"So when did you outgrow this wallflower phase?" Nick asked.

Rachel tossed a flippant grin over her shoulder. "Oh, I'm still working on it." She scurried the rest of the way up the stairs, ending up in a large sitting area that lay at the top of the landing. The hallway extended both to the left and to the right.

Making a guess, Rachel turned left and walked into a darkened room. Nick followed behind her and flipped on the light.

Oh, dear—she'd led him into the master bedroom. And it was a decidedly sensuous one at that. Decorated in shades of white and beige and cream, it almost looked like a bridal suite. The room was dominated by a massive oak bed. Filmy, sheer fabric hung like a veil from its tall, straight canopy, tied back at each of the four posters. With its mix of heavy, masculine furniture and feminine, airy fabrics, the room had an inviting, seductive air. The oversize Jacuzzi in the master bath around the corner looked far from strictly utilitarian, either.

Swallowing hard, Rachel took a step back, only to bump squarely into Nick. He reached out and caught her from behind, his hands on her waist. Even through her jacket, the feel of his hands sent a jolt of attraction racing through her.

"Sorry," she mumbled. She wasn't sure if she imagined it or if his hands actually tightened imperceptibly. She only knew that her breath froze in her throat and that his touch sent her thoughts tumbling into the past, back two and a half years to the first time he'd ever kissed her.

It had been a Saturday afternoon in January, a beautiful, warm, dry afternoon that exemplified the reason people move to Arizona. She and Nick had spent the day with several of their co-workers, climbing Squaw Mountain. Somewhere, in the course of the climb, the attraction that had been building between them for weeks at the office caught fire. Every look, every gesture, every word had seemed magnified, amplified, laden with meaning.

They'd loitered at the mountain's peak, letting the others go down before them. Nick had stood behind her. When they found themselves alone, he'd lightly rested his hands on her waist. His touch had set her heart pounding. They were yards away from the mountain's edge, but when Nick lifted her hair and kissed her on the back of the neck, she'd felt as if she were falling.

And then she'd turned around and fallen the rest of the way. When his lips had claimed hers, she'd gotten goose bumps, she'd seen stars, she'd heard waves crashing, although the ocean was hundreds of miles away.

She almost felt the same way now, just remembering it. It was both a relief and a disappointment when the baby caught sight of Nick over Rachel's shoulder and let out a wail of protest.

Nick raised his hands in a gesture of mock surrender. "Okay, okay. I promise to keep my distance, Jenny."

He made no such promise to her, Rachel noted. She could feel the heat of his gaze upon her, could feel the charge of energy in the air between them. Repositioning the baby in front of her like a shield, Rachel stepped away from him, feigning a keen interest in the decor. "What a beautiful room."

Nick gave a slow nod. "It's got definite possibilities."

The remark did nothing to put her at ease. Her legs still strangely weak, Rachel clutched Jenny and watched him prowl around like a lion inspecting his lair. He opened the drawers in the oak bureau, ran his hand across the damask upholstery of the chaise lounge in the corner, peered into the sensuous bathroom, then crossed the room to the bed. Sitting down, he gave the mattress a tentative bounce.

He looked across the room and met her gaze, his mouth curving into a slow, sexy grin. "You know, it hardly seems fair."

"What?"

"I've spent two and a half years dreaming about getting you into my bedroom. Now that I finally have, we've got a pint-size chaperone along."

Rachel felt her face flame. The temperature in the room seemed to rise, as well, and her thoughts flew back to a night two years ago when she'd nearly ended up in that very spot.

It had been a Saturday night, two months after that first kiss, two months in which they'd grown nearly inseparable. They'd spent a magical day together at the Arizona Renaissance Festival, then returned to Nick's apartment to watch a movie. As they snuggled on his leather sofa, the movie was soon forgotten as the attraction between them blazed to blow-torch intensity.

They'd been tangled in each other's arms, aroused and drugged by deep, steamy kisses and increasingly inadequate caresses. With a long, deep sigh that had sounded as if it was dredged from the bottom of his soul, Nick had reluctantly pulled away.

"I'd better take you home before we do something we'll both regret."

"What makes you think we'd regret it?" she'd whispered.

Nick had uttered a guttural groan. "You're not making this any easier." His breathing had been labored, his voice raw and raspy. He'd sat up and rubbed his jaw. "You're a forever kind of woman, Rachel, and I'm just a for-a-while kind of guy.''

''What do you mean?''

''You're the kind of woman who needs commitment and a future, and I can't offer you that.'' Sighing again, Nick had run a hand down his face. ''I'm not what you need, and I don't want to hurt you.''

''Who says you will?''

''I do. I have no interest in ever settling down. I was tied down as a kid, working on my family's farm, and when I left, I promised myself I'd never get tied down again.'' He'd looked at her, his gaze straightforward, his expression pained. ''I'm just not the settling-down type. But you…'' He'd slowly traced her cheekbone with his fingertip. ''You are.'' Rising from the sofa, he'd taken her hand and pulled her to her feet. ''Come on. I'll take you home. And from here on out, I think we'd better watch all our movies in a theater. I don't know that I'm noble enough to stop like this again.''

The creak of the bed drew her back to the present as Nick rose and walked toward her. ''Hey, I didn't mean to upset you.''

''I'm not upset.''

''Well, that bedroom crack was a lame attempt at a joke. I'm sorry. I didn't mean to embarrass you.''

It wasn't exactly embarrassment that was heating her face. The room had grown too close for comfort, too fraught with memories and emotions she'd long tried to bury.

''You didn't. It's okay.'' She pasted a smile on her face that she knew was overly bright and artificial, but it was the best she could muster under the circumstances. How, oh how was she going to manage to work with him on a daily basis, with all that had happened between them hovering in the air like a ghost?

She didn't know. She only knew she needed to guard

her heart when around him. She couldn't allow herself to indulge in memories or flights of fancy or wishful thinking. He was the same old Nick, with the same devastating charm, the same way of making her head swim and her heart race, the same way of making her futilely wish that things could be other than the way they were.

And, no doubt, the same ability to break her heart all over again.

She drew a deep breath and pushed the memories aside. "The baby's getting restless. Why don't you bring her luggage in the house while I find the nursery and change her?"

Half an hour later, Nick stood in the hallway, watching Rachel bathe the squirming baby in the bathroom.

"Wring most of the water out of the washcloth before you wash her face," Rachel directed. "Babies hate getting water in their eyes."

Nick nodded. He knew he should be paying closer attention to her play-by-play instructions so he could bathe Jenny tomorrow, but he was too absorbed in watching Rachel's graceful form stretch across the tub. She'd taken off her jacket, and as she leaned forward, he could make out the outline of a lacy bra under her tan blouse. Her pert bottom tilted up at an enticing angle, and her navy skirt was hitched up enough to reveal a lovely length of slender thigh.

Good Lord, but she was lovely. He'd forgotten exactly how lovely. Her hair was tumbling forward, exposing the back of her neck—a sight he found distinctly provocative. He remembered kissing her there, remembered how the scent of her perfume and shampoo had mingled in a heady, erotic blend.

He moved closer and leaned toward her, hoping to catch a whiff of the delicious scent now, but the baby glared up at him, wrinkled her face into an old man's frown and let out a howl of protest.

Nick rapidly backed away. "Sorry, Jenny. I didn't mean to intrude."

Rachel smiled at him over her shoulder. "A good night's rest should change her attitude."

Nicked stopped by the door. "I hope something changes it. Otherwise, the next eighteen years are going to be pretty rough."

Rachel laughed, then turned all of her attention to the baby, talking softly to the child as she finished bathing her. Nick watched Rachel lift the child out of the shallow water and wrap her in a fluffy white towel, then he followed at a distance as she carried Jenny across the hall to the white-and-ivory nursery. He stopped at the doorway, not wanting to provoke Jenny again.

Rachel really had a way with kids, he reflected, watching the way the baby smiled and laughed as Rachel powdered and diapered her. The child had devoured the dinner Rachel had spoon-fed her earlier, played happily throughout her bath and was now merrily cooperating as Rachel snapped her into a pair of Winnie-the-Pooh jammies.

"There we go," Rachel murmured. "All ready for bed."

No kidding. He'd love nothing more than to sweep Rachel off her feet and carry her off to the master bedroom.

Stop it, Delaney, he silently ordered himself. Shifting his stance, he tried to shift his thoughts, as well. "So what happens now?"

Rachel picked the baby up in her arms. "Story time. Does Jenny have any books?"

Nick nodded. "Mrs. Olsen put some in the bag with her toys. But isn't Jenny a little young for reading?"

"Babies love it. It's really good for them, too. In fact, babies that are read to from an early age are more likely to love reading when they're older."

Nick cautiously entered the room, circling around Jenny as carefully as a matador around a bull. He reached for the large suitcase that held her toys, unzipped it and pulled out a handful of colorful books. "Here you go," he said, passing them to Rachel.

"Thanks." Selecting *Goldilocks and the Three Bears,* she carried Jenny to the large white rocking chair in the corner and settled the child on her lap. Nick watched from the doorway as she softly read the story, enjoying the soothing rhythm of Rachel's voice as much as the baby.

By the end of the story, the baby's eyes had fluttered closed. Rachel gently carried the child to the crib, lowered her over the railing and tucked a small quilt around her. "Good night, sweetheart." She leaned down and kissed the baby's cheek, then raised the safety rail. "Sweet dreams."

Nick stepped aside as Rachel tiptoed through the doorway and closed the nursery door behind her. He followed her down the hall into the sitting room, shaking his head in amazement.

"That was incredible. Left to my own devices, she'd probably have kept crying until her voice gave out." He gazed at her gratefully. "I don't know how to thank you."

Rachel gave a modest shrug. "I'm glad I could help."

"Well, the least I can do is offer you dinner. I'd planned to order in a pizza."

Rachel averted her gaze. "I—I really should be going."

Nick hated the thought of her leaving. "I ruined your plans for the evening. I'd feel a lot better about taking advantage of your generosity if you'd at least share a pizza with me."

"I don't think it's a good idea."

He took a step toward her. "Look, Rachel. Since we're going to be working together, we need to get used to being around each other. It might help if we talked and cleared the air."

She drew a deep breath, then let it out in a sigh. "Okay. I suppose you're right."

Relief filled his chest. "Good. Do you still like your

pizza with green pepper, mushrooms, black olives and pepperoni?''

Rachel's lips parted in surprise. "I can't believe you remembered all that."

There was very little about Rachel that he'd forgotten, although heaven knew he'd tried. Any detail he'd managed to suppress had come rushing back in vivid detail over the last few hours—especially the full, plump curve of her bottom lip, the perfect little vee of her top lip, the way her mouth used to part when he kissed her.

He was staring again. Abruptly pulling his gaze away, he looked around for a phone. He spotted one on a table by the sofa. "Does Mario's still have the best pizza in town?"

Rachel nodded. Nick picked up the phone, silently warning himself to back off. Of all the things Rachel was making him remember, the one thing he needed to remember the most was that she was off-limits.

Rachel found herself seated beside him in the elegant sand-colored dining room an hour and a half later, a nearly empty pizza box lying on the long, gleaming table before her, enjoying herself far more than she would have thought possible. She didn't know if the wine Nick had found in the cupboard or the neutral conversation was responsible, but dinner had been far easier than she would have imagined. They'd talked about everything from work to politics to books and music.

"Have you done any traveling lately?" Nick asked, pouring the last of the wine in her glass.

"Just to Minnesota at Christmas to see my folks."

"How are they?"

"Fine. Still a pair of overprotective worrywarts, but fine."

Nick grinned companionably. "That's what you get for being an only child."

"An only child, with asthma," she reminded him. "They never quite believed I really outgrew it. One of the reasons I moved to Phoenix was because it was far enough away that my mother couldn't drive to my apartment each morning to see if I was dressed warmly enough."

Nick laughed. "You're kidding."

She rolled her eyes. "I wish I were."

Nick shook his head in amusement. "They really must have hated to see you move so far away."

Rachel nodded. "The only reason they didn't lie down in front of my moving van was because Phoenix has such a good climate. Mom thought it would be good for my health. And Dad thought it was a good career move."

Nick took a sip of wine. "You're lucky to have parents who loved you enough to let you go."

It was an odd remark. She knew Nick's mother had died while he was in college and that his father had passed away five years ago, but that was all he'd ever told her. She leaned forward, her forearms on the table. "You know, in all the time we dated, you never told me much about your parents."

A shuttered look crossed his face. "There's not much to tell," he said evasively.

He was still reluctant to talk about them. She tried another tack.

"What was it like, growing up on a farm?"

"Hard." Nick reached for his glass of wine and drained it. "A lot of hard work, a lot of hard luck. The luck factor was the thing I hated the most about it. Too many things were out of our control—rain, drought, hailstorms, insects. There were a lot of things that could go wrong, and something usually did." His glass clinked softly as he set it back on the table. "I think that's why I love dealing with numbers. They're reliable. No matter what the weather is doing, one and one is always two."

It had always struck Rachel as odd that someone as ad-

venturous as Nick had chosen a career as staid as accounting, but now she understood it. Nick needed to be in control. Come to think of it, even his most daring adventures
were situations where he remained in control.

"There must have been something you liked about growing up on a farm," Rachel prodded.

Nick shook his head grimly. "Nothing that I can think
of. That place sucked the life out of my parents. It damn
near sucked the life out of me, too, but I managed to escape.
My brother wasn't so lucky."

"What do you mean?"

"The farm had been in my family since the Oklahoma
Land Run, passed down to each eldest son, and Dad was
determined to keep it that way. He wanted me to take it
over. He said it was a family responsibility." A nerve
ticked in Nick's jaw. His eyes were flat and hard. "I didn't
want to be a farmer, didn't want to spend my life like that.
We had an argument, and I left. Unfortunately, that left my
brother saddled with the whole thing."

"He could have left, too," Rachel said softly.

Nick shook his head. "Ben never could stand up to
Dad." He shifted on his seat, then waved a hand toward
the pizza in an obvious ploy to change the topic. "Say, this
is really good. Would you like another slice?"

Rachel shook her head. "I don't think I have room for
another bite. I'm stuffed."

Nick's mouth curved in a taunting smile. "That's too
bad, because I noticed that there's some chocolate ice
cream in the freezer."

"Chocolate?" Rachel straightened and smiled. "Well,
maybe I could make just a little room for that."

Nick laughed. "You haven't changed at all." He leaned
forward. "Remember when we ordered that huge dessert
at that southside steakhouse?"

Rachel placed a hand on her stomach and moaned. "It

was enormous. Enough for five or six people. What was it called?''

"Chocolate Decadence."

Rachel nodded. "It was appropriately named."

"I remember how much you loved it." His smile grew warm.

"I remember how you spooned it into my mouth and got it all over my chin."

The heat in his eyes grew hotter. "I remember kissing a tiny smudge of chocolate off your mouth. It was right—" he reached out his hand and touched the corner of her mouth "—there."

His thumb slid across her bottom lip. His eyes held a dark, familiar light, a light that held her still and captive, a light his eyes used to get just before he kissed her.

His face was close, his voice a low, seductive rumble. "I remember that your lips were sweeter than the chocolate."

Pull back. Make yourself pull back, her mind argued with her body. With an effort, she scooted her chair slightly away from the table. "You've got a good memory." Instead of the light tone she'd intended, the words came out low and a little breathless.

"Where you're concerned, I do."

"So why did you leave?" The question that had haunted her for two years was out of her mouth before she could stop to consider the wisdom of asking it.

The question broke the seductive spell like a bucket of cold water. Nick sighed and leaned back in his chair. "I'd been offered a big advancement in my career."

"I heard you requested it."

"I did."

"So why didn't you tell me?"

"Probably for the same reason that when it was offered, I almost didn't take it."

Not take a promotion he'd requested? Nick had always

been achievement-oriented. He might take a lot of risks in his personal life, but he'd always been conservative when it came to his career. Rachel furrowed her brow. "What are you talking about?"

"I didn't want to leave you."

Rachel's heart seemed to stop in her chest. She stared at him, afraid to ask, but needing to know. Her voice came out as a hoarse whisper. "So why did you?"

"Same reason."

Time seemed suspended. The quiet was so complete, Rachel could hear the kitchen clock tick in the next room. "I—I don't understand."

Nick placed his hands on the table and sighed. "Look, Rachel—we were getting too involved. I told you at the outset that I had no intention of ever getting married, and you're not the kind of woman who would be happy with anything less. It wasn't fair to let things go any further. I hated to leave you, but I thought it was best to move on before anyone got hurt."

Then you should have moved on sooner. The thought echoed so clearly through her mind that for a moment, she thought she'd said it out loud.

She fought to keep her emotions under control, to keep the tears welling up behind her eyes from spilling out as the memory of their last day together filled her mind.

They'd spent the day hiking in Echo Canyon. The early-June weather had been perfect—warm, but not too hot, with a few high, wispy clouds in a sapphire sky. The sun had glinted off the red cliffs, making them glow like glazed terra-cotta.

A feeling of anticipation hovered in the air. All day long, Rachel had the feeling that Nick was about to say something, and with a giddy sense of anticipation, she thought she knew what it was.

He was going to propose. She'd known for weeks that she was in love with him, and she was fairly sure he felt the same way about her. Neither of them had voiced their feelings, but she was certain that was about to change. She was certain *he'd* already changed. He hadn't mentioned his aversion to matrimony in nearly two months.

Nick seemed to be biding his time that afternoon, waiting for the right moment. When he'd brought her back to her apartment, he'd leaned against the door frame and looked at her, his gaze pensive and tender, almost wistful. "It was a great day. I wish it never had to end."

"It doesn't have to," she'd whispered, opening her door. "You could come inside."

There was no mistaking what the invitation meant. With a groan of desire, he hauled her into his arms and through the door, kicking it shut behind them. His kisses were hot and hungry and fevered. His hands roamed her body, making her ache with desire. All of the restraint he'd held in place for six months melted away as he picked her up and carried her into her bedroom.

He'd placed her on the bed and leaned over her, his eyes shining and tender. She'd never forget the way he'd looked at her. He'd looked at her like a man in love. He'd opened his mouth as if he were about to say something, and then his face had taken on a stricken look. He'd suddenly hauled himself to his feet. And the next thing she knew, he'd mumbled an apology, gathered up his things and left, leaving her panting for breath, her heart aching and pounding so hard, it was a wonder it didn't bruise her ribs.

She didn't hear from him all the next day. On Monday morning, he'd called her into his office and told her he was transferring. He'd tried to tell her on Saturday, he said, but he hadn't found the right moment.

She'd sat there, stunned. They'd been interrupted by a business associate. She'd waited all day to talk to him again, but he'd been tied up in meetings. At the end of the day, she'd gone home, her heart aching, and waited for

Nick to call. He never had. And the following day, he was gone.

"I'm just not cut out for being tied down, Rachel," Nick said now.

She swallowed around a hard lump in her throat, then forced a smile that felt raw and tight. "I hate to tell you this, Nick, but having a baby to raise is going to tie you down considerably."

"Not like marriage. A baby is constantly growing and changing and becoming more independent. Marriage usually does just the opposite to people."

Where had he gotten such a bitter concept of marriage? She didn't know, but she could tell from the tone of his voice that it was a firmly held belief.

"I hate the thought of being locked into something I can never leave. The very thought of it makes me claustrophobic."

She was starting to feel claustrophobic herself, hemmed in by old thoughts and feelings and memories. She needed to get away. Her emotions were running high, and she felt dangerously close to tears.

"It—it's gotten late. I'd better take a rain check on that ice cream." She rose from her chair, picked up her purse and rapidly headed for the foyer.

Nick put his hand on her arm, stopping her at the front door. "Hey—there's no reason to rush off."

"If I hurry, I might be able to catch up with Patricia for the second half of the double feature."

She could feel his eyes on her as she fiddled in her purse for her keys. She was sure he didn't believe the flimsy excuse, but she was grateful he didn't call her on it.

"I'll walk you to your car," he said.

"There's no need. Stay inside where you can listen for the baby."

He was still holding her arm. His hand was warm on her skin, but his eyes were warmer still. "Well, thanks for your help with Jenny. I can't tell you how much I appreciate it.''

It took every ounce of her strength to manage a smile. ''That's what old friends are for.''

He opened the door, and she hurried through it, her head ducked down.

Old friends, he thought ruefully, watching her go. Was that what she thought they were? The casual label inexplicably stung.

But what else were they? They'd never been lovers.

The whole damn situation probably would have been easier if they had. At least then it would be a familiar scenario. He didn't quite know how to act around her. He'd intended to clear the air, but instead he'd only muddied the water.

He watched from the doorway as she climbed in her car, backed it out of the driveway and drove off down the street. He watched until her taillights faded in the distance, then disappeared around a corner.

Old friends. He pulled his forehead into a scowl, not understanding why her remark bothered him so. It was what he'd wanted, wasn't it? A pleasant, platonic relationship. So why the hell did the thought of being friends with Rachel leave him feeling as if he'd just been served a stalk of celery when what he was hungry for was a steak dinner?

Chapter Three

The shrill ring of the telephone awakened Rachel the next morning. Groggy and still half-asleep, she opened her eyes, winced against the morning light filtering through the muted floral curtains of her bedroom window and glanced at the alarm clock on her nightstand.

Seven o'clock. Who would be calling her at this hour on a Saturday? Without lifting her head from the pillow, she reached out and grabbed the phone in the middle of the second ring.

"Hello?"

"Rachel, it's Nick."

Her pulse immediately accelerated. She abruptly sat up in bed, clutching the phone in one hand, brushing her hair out of her face with the other. The loud wail of a baby shrieked through the receiver. "I hear Jenny. Is something wrong?"

"She woke up at three, and she's been crying ever since. I've tried everything I could think of to calm her down. I changed her diaper, I gave her a bottle, I rocked her in the rocking chair. I burped her and sang to her and carried her around the house. I even got out her stroller and wheeled her around the kitchen. Nothing works.'' He sounded frazzled and worried. "I hate bothering you, but I don't know what to do.''

"Does she have a fever?''

"I don't know.''

"Well, does she feel hot?''

"I don't think so, but I'm not a good judge of these things. Her face is awfully red, but that might be because she's been crying so hard for so long.''

"Do you have a thermometer?''

"No. But even if I did, I know just enough about how to take a baby's temperature to know I don't dare try it.'' Jenny's crying switched to a higher pitch. "Rachel, what should I do?''

The baby sounded frantic, and so did Nick.

Rachel sighed. "I'll be right over.''

She threw off the covers and swung her feet to the floor, emotions warring inside of her, the same emotions that had kept her tossing and turning for much of the night. It was a mistake to go back over there, especially now that she knew that Nick had left two years ago because they'd grown too close.

It was a mistake, because a piece of her heart rejoiced in that knowledge.

She'd spent the past two years wondering why he'd left so suddenly, wondering if she'd deluded herself about his degree of emotional involvement with her, wondering if she'd been so head over heels in love that she hadn't accurately judged his true feelings for her. Perhaps she'd misread his signals. Perhaps he'd never been as attracted to her as she was to him, never cared for her as she'd cared for him. Perhaps he'd simply grown tired of her and found it was easier to move on than to break up with her since she was a co-worker.

But she hadn't been wrong. He *had* cared for her. The

reason he hadn't made love to her was not because he didn't desire her, but because he didn't want to hurt her. A tender, honorable part of Nick had been respecting her dreams and protecting her heart.

But then there was the flip side of him. He had a deep-seated aversion to permanence. He'd told her again last night that he had no intention of ever marrying. Time had passed, but nothing had changed.

Nothing except for Jenny. The thought of the poor, orphaned baby inconsolably crying propelled Rachel off the bed and into the shower.

When she pulled her car into Nick's driveway thirty minutes later, he and Jenny were waiting for her on the front porch.

Rachel's heart turned over at the sight of them. Unshaven and red-eyed, the normally well-groomed Nick wore rumpled navy sweatpants and a stained T-shirt, and looked as distraught as Jenny sounded. Rachel had never seen two more miserable-looking human beings in her life.

Nick met her halfway up the sidewalk, carrying the red-faced, howling baby. "Thank heavens you're here."

Jenny strained her chubby arms toward Rachel, her tiny face red and wrinkled as a baked apple. Rachel lifted the child into her arms, cradling her head against her shoulder.

"Hey, there, sweetie pie," Rachel said soothingly. "What's the matter?"

"She's in the custody of an incompetent, that's what's the matter." Nick's mouth curved in a rueful smile, but his eyes were full of worry.

Rachel's urge to comfort Nick was nearly as strong as her urge to comfort Jenny. "She's probably just missing her parents."

"What if it's something more?" Nick's brow wrinkled in concern. "What if she's sick and we just don't know it?"

Rachel felt the child's forehead. "She doesn't feel feverish, but it would probably be a good idea to take her to a pediatrician and get her checked out all the same.''

"Any idea how to find a pediatrician?''

Rachel nodded. "I've got a friend in the legal department who's pregnant. Olivia has interviewed half of the children's doctors in Phoenix, trying to find the right one for her baby. I'll give her a call.''

"Thanks a million, Rachel.''

The gratitude in his olive eyes sent a rush of warmth through her chest. She abruptly turned away, steeling herself against the pull of attraction she felt for him. "I'm glad to help.''

But she was secretly glad of more than that. She was glad to be needed, glad of an excuse to be here with him and Jenny again.

The realization dismayed her. She didn't want any emotional ties to Nick. She'd hoped that time had loosened the hold he had on her, but the wild pounding of her heart warned her otherwise.

"Hello. I'm Dr. Jackson.''

Nick rose from the straight-backed chair as the gray-haired pediatrician entered the examining room.

The man's kindly face folded into a smile as he shook Nick's hand, glancing at the medical chart in his hand. "Nice to meet you, Mr. Delaney.'' He nodded amiably at Rachel, who was seated across the room with Jenny on her lap. "Mrs. Delaney.''

"Oh, no,'' Rachel blurted. "I mean, we're not married.''

The doctor closed the door behind him, doing an admirable job of squelching the surprise on his face. "I'm sorry. I shouldn't jump to conclusions like that in this day and age.'' He turned his attention to Jenny, who was still sitting on Rachel's lap. "Hello there, young lady. You must be Jenny.''

Jenny turned her head against Rachel's shoulder and whimpered.

"A shy one, eh?" the doctor remarked. "Are you the child's mother?"

Rachel's face flamed beet-red. "No."

The doctor turned to Nick, his eyebrows raised in confusion. "I seem to be striking out all around. Then you must be the child's father."

Nick shifted uncomfortably. "Well, not exactly."

The doctor all but scratched his head.

"She's my niece," Nick hurried to explain. "My brother and his wife were killed in an auto accident, and I'm her new legal guardian. Problem is, ever since I've been taking care of her, all she does is cry. She's always been finicky about anyone except her parents caring for her, but ever since they died, she's been impossible. She won't let me feed her or hold her or comfort her in any way. In fact, she won't tolerate anyone coming close to her except Rachel here."

"I see." The doctor looked again at Rachel. "And Rachel is…?"

Crimony—how was he supposed to describe his relationship with Rachel? He fell back on the phrase he'd so hated the night before. "An old friend—a very close old friend. Jenny and I have just moved to Phoenix, and Rachel's helping us out until I can hire a nanny."

"I see." The doctor turned to Rachel and smiled. "Well, let's start by ruling out any physical reasons for Jenny's distress."

Rachel carried the child to the examining table. Jenny wailed the moment the doctor approached her. Dr. Jackson peered over his glasses at Rachel. "If you don't mind, it might help if you hold her while I examine her."

"Of course."

Nick watched, feeling completely useless, as Rachel sat on the table and held the whimpering baby in her arms while the doctor checked the child's ears, eyes, nose and throat. At the doctor's instructions, Rachel stretched the child on the table and talked to her soothingly as he felt Jenny's stomach, checked her legs and examined her diaper area. When he'd finished his examination, he handed the outraged infant back to Rachel.

Dr. Jackson watched thoughtfully as Jenny calmed down almost immediately once she was back in Rachel's arms.

"Well?" Nick prompted.

"She seems to be perfectly healthy." Dr. Jackson removed his spectacles and regarded Nick calmly. "I'd guess that she's grieving the loss of her parents."

Nick raised his eyebrows in surprise. "Babies can experience grief?"

The doctor nodded. "Oh, yes. They begin to recognize their parents' voices while they're still in the womb, and they form attachments very early. Like adults, different babies cope with loss and change in different ways." The doctor eyed Nick speculatively. "Babies are sometimes confused by the way an unfamiliar relative can look or even smell like a lost parent. It's not inconceivable that Jenny is rejecting you because you remind her of her missing father."

Nick frowned. "You mean I make her miss him more?"

The doctor nodded. "She might be angry that you're so much like her daddy, yet you're not him."

Nick ran a frustrated hand through his hair. "What do you recommend I do?"

The doctor lowered himself onto a backless stool by the examining table, his face serious. "You need to ease the baby's transition to her new home and new environment as much as possible. She has to get used to you gradually. The best way to do that is to let someone she trusts, like Rachel here, care for her while she gets accustomed to being around you."

A surge of alarm rushed through Nick. It was bad enough

that he'd turned to Rachel twice in less than twenty-four hours. He didn't want to involve her any further. "I intend to hire a daytime nanny as soon as possible. In fact, I'm hoping to do that today."

The doctor frowned. "I don't recommend introducing another new person right now. From what you've told me, the child has a hard time adjusting to a change in caregivers under the best of circumstances, and Jenny is confused and upset enough as it is. Since she's obviously comfortable with Rachel, the ideal situation would be to have Rachel stay in your home and care for the baby around the clock while Jenny grows to accept you."

No way. He hated taking help from anyone, but especially from Rachel. She'd already done more than enough as it was. He didn't want to feel indebted, didn't want to feel dependent. Most of all, he didn't want to feel like he needed her.

Nick glanced at Rachel. Her eyes were fixed straight ahead, but her face looked paler than usual.

"I know it's a lot to ask of a friend," Dr. Jackson continued. "I don't know your circumstances or the nature of your relationship, but it would be in the baby's best interests."

"How long do you think it would take?" Rachel asked.

"There's no way to say exactly, but I would think that about a week would probably do it."

Nick shook his head. "I don't want to impose on Rachel any further. What are the alternatives?"

The doctor stroked his chin. "Well, you could try finding a nanny Jenny can relate to, but if the baby is as sensitive to strangers as you say, you're likely to have a situation where the baby rejects you both." The doctor perched his glasses back on his nose. "I had a similar case with an adopted infant a few years ago. The child ended up having to be hospitalized for dehydration because she refused to eat or drink."

"Oh, Nick—we can't let that happen to Jenny," Rachel murmured.

"In any event," the doctor continued, "regardless of who you use as an interim caregiver, you're going to need to be around the child almost continually for the next week or so, Mr. Delaney, in order for the primary relationship between you and the baby to have a chance to form."

Nick frowned. "You mean I need to stay home from work in order to bond with the baby?"

The doctor smiled mildly. "Unless you and your caregiver can take the child to your place of work."

"I'm sure Rex wouldn't mind, especially under the circumstances," Rachel said. "Several employees have brought their children to the office when their child-care arrangements fell through. It's up to the discretion of the divisional vice president. In this case, that's you."

The doctor regarded them curiously. "I take it you two work together?"

Nick nodded.

"Then I'd say the situation is just about ideal." The doctor grinned and rose from the stool. "I'd like to see Jenny again in two weeks. Tell the receptionist to schedule a well-baby appointment, and be sure to bring all of her immunization records." He walked to the door and hesitated, his hand on the handle. "For the baby's sake, I hope you can talk Rachel here into giving you a hand for the next week or so. If not, keep an eye on how long the child goes without taking in any liquids. Babies dehydrate a lot faster than adults. If she goes more than twenty-four hours without consuming any fluids, bring her back and let me check her."

The whole situation sounded frighteningly serious. Nick shook his head as the doctor closed the examining room door behind him.

"We won't let anything happen to Jenny," Rachel said

firmly, boosting the baby higher on her shoulder. "I'll stay and take care of her."

What was she saying? a voice deep inside her demanded. *After just one evening with Nick, she'd been an emotional basket case. What would a whole week do to her?*

Rachel didn't know, and at the moment, she didn't care. She only cared about Jenny. The baby needed her, and that was what counted.

Nick shoved his hands in his pockets, the way he always did when he was ill at ease. "Look, I don't want to drag you into this. It's unfair to put you on the spot just because you were kind enough to come help me out this morning."

Nick was the one who was on the spot, Rachel thought. He'd lost his brother and sister-in-law, he'd suddenly become the parent of a very needy baby, he'd just made a major move and he was due to start a new, demanding job on Monday. It was almost too much for one person to deal with alone.

But Nick didn't want to accept any further help from her. She could see it in the stubborn set of his jaw. Was he, too, afraid of spending too much time alone with her? The thought made her pulse quicken.

"You've been very kind, but you've done more than enough already," Nick continued.

"I'm not offering to help you. I'm offering to help Jenny." Rachel looked directly into his eyes. "The doctor said it would be in her best interests. Are you going to refuse to follow Jenny's doctor's orders because you're too proud and stubborn?"

She could almost see the battle within him. He gazed at the baby, then looked back at her.

She gave her most persuasive smile. "I love babies. Let me help Jenny."

She saw him swallow, then slowly nod. "Thanks, Rachel," he said softly. "Thanks a million."

* * *

Rachel refolded a pair of jeans for the second time, deliberately dawdling as she unpacked her suitcase in Nick's guest room. The longer she took putting her things away, the longer she could postpone going downstairs.

It was unnerving enough, being in the same room with Nick when Jenny was present. But now that their tiny chaperone was taking a midday nap, they would be alone.

Spending time alone with Nick was an inevitable consequence of staying in his home, of course. On some level she'd known that when she'd volunteered to help him out, but she hadn't allowed herself to really think about it.

They'd driven to her apartment after they'd left the doctor's office so that she could collect her things. She'd quickly packed a couple of bags while Jenny played on a blanket on the bedroom floor. Nick had watched from the bedroom doorway.

It had felt odd, having Nick in her place again—especially in her bedroom. She couldn't help but remember the night he'd carried her in there, the night she'd wanted to give him her heart and soul and body.

The night he'd walked out on her.

The memories had made her feel overheated and overwrought. As a result, she'd thrown clothes into her suitcase so rapidly, she wasn't quite sure what she'd packed.

Once they'd arrived at Nick's house, she'd kept her attention tightly focused on Jenny. As Nick watched, she'd fed Jenny, changed her, given her an extra bottle of juice, then rocked her to sleep for a much-needed nap. Rachel had then fled to the safety of her bedroom.

A knock sounded on her door. Tucking the folded jeans into an empty bureau drawer, Rachel crossed the room and opened it. Nick stood in the doorway, wearing a boyish grin. To her chagrin, her heart sped up at the sight of him.

"I've made some lunch. Come and get it."

She opened her mouth to make an excuse, then abruptly closed it. She'd been in such a hurry to get to Nick's place this morning that she'd skipped breakfast. She was famished. Besides, she couldn't spend the whole week hiding out in the guest room. She needed to get comfortable around Nick or at least learn to act as if she was. Either way, it would be good practice for working with him again.

Forcing a smile, she reached for the portable baby monitor and clipped it onto the pocket of her jeans. "Great. I'm starved."

She followed him down the stairs and into the breakfast nook where two places were set side by side at the oval oak table by the window.

"We're having the chef's specialty—sandwiches and potato chips," Nick announced. "It's the specialty because it's the only thing the chef knows how to cook."

Rachel smiled. "I'm certain the chef will be adding creamed peas and puréed carrots to his repertoire before you know it."

"That's true. I'm already working on mashed bananas and squashed peaches for this establishment's most finicky patron." Grinning broadly, Nick pulled out a chair. Rachel seated herself in it, feeling a bit self-conscious at his gallantry. She'd always loved Nick's impeccable manners, had always thought there was a subtle sexiness to the way he'd open a door for her or pull out her chair. It was such a male-female thing—a small but frequent reminder that he was a man, she was a woman and he recognized and appreciated the differences between them.

Not that she'd ever needed a reminder. Being around Nick had always put her in a state of heightened sexual awareness.

She was uncomfortably aware right now. Not wanting to show it, she unfolded her napkin, placed it on her lap and eyed the plate with a show of interest. "Sliced turkey—my favorite."

"I remember." Nick's eyes locked on hers, and a shiver

of awareness skittered up her arm. "I fixed it just the way you like it, with mayonnaise and mustard mixed together."

The fact that he remembered such a small detail unnerved her. "And I suppose you have ketchup on yours," she countered.

"You bet." He leaned forward, his eyes glittering. "It's funny what you remember, isn't it?"

The conversation was becoming disturbingly intimate. She gave a hesitant nod, then reached for her glass of iced tea, searching for a way to steer it to a safer subject. "It was interesting, what Dr. Jackson said about you reminding Jenny of her father. Were you and Ben much alike?"

Nick lifted his shoulders. "We looked alike, but otherwise we were pretty much complete opposites."

"What do you mean?"

"Ben was quiet and complacent, and I was the family rebel."

The information made Rachel lean forward. "What did you rebel against?"

"My father, mostly."

"Why? Was he strict?"

"'Strict' doesn't begin to describe it." Nick's mouth flattened into a tight, hard line. "Try domineering, dictatorial, autocratic and unreasonable." He picked up his sandwich again. "It's not something I like to talk about."

"So I gathered." Rachel took a sip of iced tea and watched him take a bite of sandwich. "You never told me anything about your childhood."

Nick swallowed hard, as if his sandwich had just turned bitter. "That's because there wasn't much of it."

"What do you mean?"

"Ben and I grew up buried in chores. Not just chores that were necessary for the operation of the farm, but busywork that Dad dreamed up to keep us from doing anything else."

Rachel's eyebrows rose in surprise. "Why did your father do that?"

Nick shrugged, his expression grim. "I think he thought that if we were ever exposed to another way of life, we'd want to leave. He did everything he could to keep us home."

"But why?"

"He was obsessed with keeping the farm in the family. I knew from an early age that I didn't want to be a farmer, but Dad refused to even listen. Since I was the eldest son, I was supposed to run it, and that was that. By the time I was a teenager, he'd given up trying to talk me into it and had started trying to force me."

"How?"

"Mostly by limiting my options. He wouldn't let me have any kind of social life. He wouldn't let me join the high school football team or debate team. He said I had too many chores. I could have been on the teams and done my chores, too, but he wouldn't even let me try." Nick stared out at the manicured backyard and blew out a harsh breath. For a long moment, Rachel wondered if he were going to continue.

"When I was a senior, I won an all-expense-paid trip to Washington, D.C.," he finally said. "I was supposed to represent my school in an honors math competition, but Dad wouldn't let me go. He said I didn't need to know any more math than it took to run the farm."

"Oh, Nick," Rachel breathed, her brow knit in concern.

"Mom tried to change his mind, but he wouldn't budge. He said it would do nothing but give me a lot of high falutin big ideas."

Rachel searched her mind for something, anything encouraging to say. "At least your mom sounds sympathetic."

Nick nodded. "She was—when she wasn't drowning her troubles in a bottle. She'd given up her dream of being an artist when she married Dad, and she'd always regretted it."

"Did she and your father get along?"

Nick shook his head. "No. My father made her miserable, and she did the best she could to return the favor." He gave a bitter smile. "My folks weren't exactly Ozzie and Harriet. I asked Mom once why she didn't leave. She told me she'd made a sacred vow, and she had to honor it no matter what."

No wonder Nick had such a terrible impression of marriage and family life, Rachel thought. "Mom didn't want me to end up like her. She urged me to follow my dreams and encouraged me to apply for a college scholarship." He gave a tight grin. "When I won one, Dad went ballistic. His face got so red and mottled that I thought he was going to have a stroke. He tried to bully me into staying. He said that if I left, I could never come back."

Rachel reached out and placed her hand on top of his. He turned his hand and folded her fingers into his own. "I don't think he believed I'd call his bluff. When I told him I was going anyway, he threw me out of the house with just the clothes on my back. I spent the night sleeping in a ditch beside the road."

"How awful."

"That's not the worst of it. He forbade me to ever talk to my mother or brother again. He said that if he found out they'd been in contact with me, he'd throw them out without a dime, too."

Rachel gasped.

"The horrible thing was, we all knew he meant it." Nick exhaled heavily. "Mom died a year later. She used to write to me behind Dad's back, and I'd call her when I knew Dad would be out in the fields, but I never saw her alive again."

"What happened to your brother?"

"Ben stayed home and worked the farm." His fingers

tensed around Rachel's hand. "We used to talk about sailing around the world together and hiking the Himalayas and having all kinds of great adventures. But he never went anywhere or did anything or knew much of anything except the farm." Nick glanced away. Rachel saw a muscle flex in his jaw. "He took on the role I refused to fill. If I had stayed, maybe Ben would have gotten to have a life."

"But he *did* have a life," Rachel softly pointed out. "He got married and had Jenny."

"Yeah, but he never got to pursue his dreams."

"Maybe he did."

Nick looked up at her, his eyes questioning.

"Maybe his dreams changed."

Rachel could tell Nick didn't believe that. Of course he wouldn't, she thought sadly. In Nick's mind, marriage was a lifelong jail sentence.

His face grew determined. "All I know is this—I'm going to make sure Jenny has the chance to become anything she wants to be."

Rachel gave him an encouraging smile. "You're going to do a great job with her."

"I sure want to. But my credentials in the relationship department are pretty poor." He looked at Rachel, his mouth curved in a sad smile. "You of all people should know that."

Ignoring the pounding of her heart, Rachel searched for words to encourage him. "You'll be terrific. You're warm and affectionate and you have a great sense of fun. Heck, you can even make monthly profit and loss reports seem like fun. Imagine what you can do for ABCs and one-two-threes." She squeezed his hand and gave him an encouraging smile. "Jenny's lucky to have you. You have a gift for enjoying life and for helping other people enjoy it, too."

Nick looked unconvinced. "Sounds more like the criteria for becoming a clown than raising a child."

"I don't think so," Rachel said softly. "I think it sounds

like a man who'll do a great job teaching a child how to enjoy reaching her full potential.''

Nick reached out and touched her cheek, his lips curved in a smile. "You've always had a way of making me feel better about things, Rachel.''

She smiled back at him. He'd never known blue could be such a warm color, he thought distractedly, gazing into her eyes. His thumb slid across her cheek. He'd never known skin could be so soft, either. And he'd never seen anything as tempting as Rachel's lips. They were pink and moist and slightly parted, and he couldn't help but remember how they'd tasted.

It was almost as if she read his thoughts. He saw her eyes widen, saw her pupils dilate, saw the attraction flare in response to his own. He tightened his grip on her hand, and she returned the pressure.

He'd sworn to himself that he would be a perfect gentleman, that he would adhere to a strict hands-off policy while she was a guest in his home, but he found himself leaning toward her, pulled by a force as powerful and elemental as gravity. His hand reached around the back of her head. Her hair was even softer than he remembered, soft and springy and satin textured. He sifted it through his fingers. Her eyes locked on his. He'd intended to pull her toward him, but she was moving that way on her own.

He didn't want to rush her, but the anticipation was killing him. His breath caught in his throat. Her lips were six inches, five inches, now four inches from his own.

And then a familiar, high-pitched cry crackled through the baby monitor on the kitchen counter.

Nick heard Rachel's sharp intake of breath, felt her pull back. Reluctantly he released her and straightened.

Her eyes were wide and alarmed, like a sleepwalker who'd just awakened to discover herself in an expected place. "I—I'd better go check on Jenny." Rachel's chair screeched on the tile floor as she jumped to her feet and fled the room.

Chapter Four

Rachel knelt over him, her hair caressing his face, the mahogany-colored strands smooth and feather soft and fragrant. Her hair moved over him, draping across his chest like a satin sheet, grazing his cheek, filtering through his fingers, soft as moonlight. She was teasing him, deliberately taunting him—so near, yet just out of reach. He could nearly claim her lips, nearly feel the warmth of her body. He wanted her—desperately, achingly, painfully. He reached out to draw her down against him, and then...

The loud wail of a baby burst into Nick's dream like a rude intruder. Jerking his eyes open, Nick sat up in bed and glanced at the alarm clock on his nightside table—4:53 a.m.

Crimony. What was the baby doing up at this hour?

Down the hall, a door creaked open. He heard the soft patter of feet, then the squeak of another door.

Rachel. The details of his dream were floating away from him, breaking up and trailing off like a wispy, fading cloud, but the thought of her here, in his house, sent another pulse of desire racing through him.

Nick swung his feet to the floor. No wonder he was

having erotic dreams, he thought disgruntedly. He'd been thinking of nothing but Rachel ever since he'd nearly kissed her at lunch yesterday.

No, ever since *she'd* nearly kissed *him*, he mentally corrected himself. That was what he couldn't get off his mind. She'd been just as willing, just as tempted as he was. If the baby hadn't interrupted, there was no telling where they would have ended up. Maybe, he thought, looking around his frankly sensuous bedroom, even in here.

The thought did nothing to cool him off. With a mumbled oath, Nick rose and adjusted his navy sweatpants. He didn't bother to pull on a shirt. He was plenty warm as it was.

He hurried into the nursery to find Rachel at the changing table, taping a new diaper on Jenny. "Is she okay?"

"She was a little soggy, but in these superabsorbent diapers, I doubt she even knew it."

"So why was she crying?"

"Probably because she thinks it's time to get up." Rachel's hair hung loose around her shoulders, reminding him of how it had flowed about her face in the dream. She wore a rose-colored satin robe, and the way she self-consciously tightened it made him wonder what she was—or wasn't—wearing underneath it.

The thought made him irritable. "Well, she's mistaken," he grumbled. "All self-respecting people stay in bed until at least six o'clock. Especially on Sunday mornings."

Rachel grinned as she resnapped the baby's pajamas. "Not according to Jenny. And she gets to call the shots."

"Seniority doesn't count for anything?"

"Not as far as Jenny is concerned." Rachel smiled at him. "Could you watch her for a moment while I go wash my hands?"

"Sure."

Nick cautiously approached the changing table and gazed

down at the baby. "Good morning, kiddo. Remember me?"

The baby's forehead wrinkled into a frown. She stuck her fist in her mouth and whimpered unhappily.

"I see that you do." Disheartened, Nick took a step back. The baby whined and eyed him warily, but at least she didn't burst into a full-lunged howl.

"You're making progress," Rachel remarked, reentering the room. "She's letting you stand closer than yesterday."

"Maybe so, but she's not happy about it."

"It's progress all the same."

Unfortunately, he thought grimly, he wasn't making any progress with Rachel—not in the direction he needed to be moving, at least. He'd come back to Arizona determined to develop a purely platonic, strictly professional relationship with her, and what had he done instead? He'd moved her into his home, become heavily dependent on her and started having erotic dreams about her.

The neck of her robe gaped open as she bent to pick up Jenny. He caught a glimpse of her surprisingly lush décolletage and immediately felt a surge of desire.

Dammit, it wasn't helping matters that they were both standing there in their nightclothes. "Why don't we get dressed, then go downstairs and fix some breakfast?"

"I think we're going to have to see to Jenny's breakfast first," Rachel said, smiling at the baby. "Judging from the way she's about to devour her fist, I'd say we have about five minutes to get her some food or suffer the consequences." Rachel glanced up at him. "But you can go ahead and change if you want to."

He needed a cold shower in the worst way, but he wasn't going to cop out. "Nah. The doctor said the more I'm around Jenny, the sooner she'll learn to tolerate me." And the sooner Rachel would stop playing such a giant role in his life.

He pondered the situation as he followed her down the

stairs. Jenny stared at him over Rachel's shoulder, regarding him with frank distrust.

He needed a way to win the baby over. The technique he usually used with a female was to show her a good time and get her to let down her guard. Maybe it would work on Jenny, as well.

"What do babies do for fun?" he asked.

Rachel's eyebrows arched in surprise. "I think just about everything is fun for a baby."

"What things do they like the most?" he persisted, following her into the kitchen.

"Well, they like to play with all kinds of toys. They like to swing. And most babies love to play in water."

Water—that was it!

"I've got an idea," Nick said leaning against the counter. "Jenny really seemed to like playing in the bathtub last night. After breakfast, let's get one of those little wading pools for the backyard."

Several hours later, Nick stood on the back lawn, using a bicycle pump to pump air into an inflatable pool, while Jenny and Rachel changed into their swimsuits. At Rachel's suggestion, he'd already pulled Jenny's high chair out onto the deck and set it at the large umbrella-covered table, next to four wrought-iron chairs covered with colorful cushions. He'd also set up Jenny's portable crib in the shade of the deck, and spread a blanket on the lawn for sunbathing.

It had been a busy morning. The three of them had made a trip to the local Wal-Mart and nearly cleaned out the store's water-toy supply. On the way back, they'd swung by Rachel's apartment to let her get her swimsuit.

He heard the French door that led from the breakfast room to the deck swing open, and rapidly turned around, eager to see Rachel in the scrap of red Spandex she'd toted out to the car. He was disappointed to discover she was wearing a long, loose T-shirt over it. The legs that the shirt exposed were no disappointment, however. Long and lean and smooth, they were exactly as he remembered.

She was holding Jenny, who looked plump as a baby seal in her new hot-pink swimsuit. A pink sun hat and matching sunglasses with yellow ducks on the cat's-eye corners completed Jenny's beach wear ensemble.

Nick grinned. "She looks like a link sausage in that swimsuit."

Rachel laughed. "She's adorable, isn't she?"

"Both of you are. But you're a whole lot less sausage-like."

He liked the way Rachel blushed. He'd forgotten how easily he could make her do it. It was one of the things he'd always loved about her.

Liked, he mentally corrected himself. He never used the word *love* in connection with a woman.

He gave the bicycle pump a few extra pushes, then disconnected it and punched the plastic stopper into the air hole. "We're ready to fill this thing up. I think I saw a garden hose in the garage."

He filled up a pair of water guns while he was at it, then returned to find Rachel seated by the umbrella-covered table, carefully dabbing sunblock on Jenny as the baby sat in her lap. "You seem to have thought of everything," he said, lowering himself into the chair beside them.

"Babies have really sensitive skin. Whenever Jenny's going to be out in the sun for any length of time, you'll need to put sunblock on her."

"There's an awful lot to this parenthood business," Nick said, shaking his head. "I don't know if I'll ever remember it all."

"Sure you will." In the bright sunlight, her eyes were as blue as the sky. "I have faith in you."

The words did something dangerously tender to his heart. He gazed at her, and their eyes locked. Time hung in the air, suddenly unimportant.

Jenny reached for the bottle of sunblock. Rachel pulled it away from her, then nervously scrambled to her feet. "I'd better get this baby some milk before she tries to drink the sunblock." She scooped up the child and fastened her into the high chair Nick had brought out earlier. "If you'll watch her, I'll bring out lunch."

"What's Jenny having?"

"Puréed carrots."

Making a face, Nick looked down at the baby as Rachel left. "You need to grow some more teeth, kiddo, so you can graduate to the good stuff."

Jenny somberly regarded him for a long moment, and then her mouth curved into an expression that might have been a slight smile. Just as quickly as it appeared, it was gone. But Nick's heart soared in a way it hadn't done in years.

He leaned forward. "Hey, kiddo, did you just smile at me?"

The baby stuck her fist in her mouth and stared. She didn't repeat the performance, but at least she wasn't crying.

"I think she smiled at me!" Nick proudly announced when Rachel returned.

"That's great." Smiling warmly, Rachel set the tray on the patio table and turned to the baby. "Are you making friends with your daddy?" she asked, reaching forward to tousle Jenny's curly blond hair.

Daddy. The word hit him like a pipe bomb. It was emotionally loaded, psychologically explosive.

He knew it was irrational, but something about it scared him to death. Fatherhood was serious business—as grim and serious as his own father had been.

"Ben was her daddy." Nick's voice came out unusually low and gruff. "I can't ever take his place, and I don't want to pretend I can."

Surprise flickered across Rachel's face. She gazed at him

searchingly. "Well, then, what do you want Jenny to call you?"

Hell, he hadn't thought of that. He shifted his stance and rubbed a hand across his bare chest. "I'm her uncle, so Uncle Nick, I guess."

Concern etched lines around Rachel's eyes. She looked as if she were about to say something, then evidently changed her mind. Nick didn't press her. He had a feeling he wouldn't agree with her thoughts on the subject.

He watched her tie a yellow Big Bird bib around the child's neck, then sit down on the opposite side of Jenny.

"Ready to try some carrots?" Rachel asked. The baby gurgled gleefully, and Rachel spooned a mouthful of orange mush into the child's mouth.

Jenny's eyes grew round as blue moons at the taste of the new food. Her nose wrinkled and her forehead puckered.

"Look at that face! She looks like a troll doll." Nick leaned forward and grinned. "So what do you think, Jenny? Do you like carrots or not?"

As if in response, Jenny spewed orange goo all over Nick's bare chest.

Nick reflexively jerked back. The baby burst into a fit of orange-mouthed giggles.

She was smiling at him. Jenny was looking straight at him, and indisputably smiling.

He glanced at Rachel. "Do you see that?"

Rachel nodded, her eyes soft and shining.

It was a miraculous feeling, making the baby laugh. Nick couldn't wait to do it again.

He stared down at his chest, feigning an expression of stupefied surprise. Jenny laughed all the harder. He viewed her in wide-eyed alarm, then donned the manner of a snobbish maitre d'. "Was zee dish not to mademoiselle's liking?"

A fresh round of giggles greeted his performance.

"Here at Château de BéBé, we maintain only zee highest

standards. If mademoiselle doesn't like zee carrots, why, zee carrots shall disappear. Voilà." He placed a paper napkin on top of the bowl of carrots on her tray.

Grinning with delight, Jenny tugged the napkin away.

"Oh, no no no no no," Nick said, still speaking in the pompous accent. "Zee offending carrots must go." Once more he covered the bowl. Once more Jenny snatched at the napkin, delighted at this unexpected game of hide-and-seek.

After a few more rounds, Nick pretended to surrender. "Perhaps I made zee colossal boo-boo. It seems as if mademoiselle would like zee carrots to remain after all. I will leave them for mademoiselle's future dining pleasure. In the meantime, I'd better get cleaned up." Reaching across the table, Nick picked up one of the loaded water pistols. Making a face like Stan Laurel, he aimed it at his chest and squirted.

Jenny banged her high chair tray in merriment. Rachel laughed, too.

"Well, at least I've figured out how to win her over," Nick remarked.

"Continually dribble smooshed carrots?" Rachel asked.

Nick grinned. "That wasn't exactly what I meant."

"Become a fashion trendsetter and start a line of chest hair accessories?"

Nick laughed aloud. "That wasn't what I had in mind, either, but it's an original idea."

"Hmm. Maybe you were thinking of opening a restaurant that specializes in wearable cuisine?"

Nick had forgotten how much he missed this—the humorous back-and-forth banter, the way Rachel could not only enjoy his silly pranks, but could make him laugh in return. He sometimes used to feel as if they were a private comedy team, completely in sync, playing to an audience of only themselves.

And to Jenny, now, too, Nick thought, gazing at the giggling baby. She couldn't understand the exchange, but she seemed completely willing to join in all the same. Grinning like a gap-toothed monkey, she clumsily slapped at her tray and cooed.

Nick grinned. "I was going to say that Jenny only seems to like me when I'm making a complete fool of myself."

"Well, of course," Rachel teased. "What female can resist a man who's making a fool of himself on her behalf?"

"Is *that* the secret?" Nick smacked his forehead with the palm of his hand. "In that case..." Crossing his eyes, Nick comically toppled out of his chair.

Rachel laughed, and Jenny did, too.

There was something golden about the moment, something rich and real and rare that made Nick wish he could somehow package this slice of time and keep it forever. He didn't know what, exactly, made it seem so right. Probably not any one thing. Like a favorite dish, it was probably a blending of all the right ingredients—the sunshine, the baby's smile, the laughter and...Rachel.

Most definitely Rachel. Good Lord, but he'd missed her. He hadn't allowed himself to admit it, not until this moment. But he had. He'd missed her. More than he was comfortable acknowledging.

He looked at her as he picked himself up and reseated himself in the chair. The sun was behind her, forming a golden aureola around her, highlighting golden streaks in her hair, backlighting her like a halo. She looked like an angel—a blue-eyed, soft-smiling angel. "You know, I could make a fool of myself over you pretty easily," he found himself saying.

Rachel's eyes widened. Awareness crackled in the air between them. And for a moment, everything seemed on the verge of changing.

And then Rachel grabbed the second pistol from the table. "You want to make a fool of yourself? Here, let me help." With a mischievous grin, she aimed and fired, hitting him squarely on the side of the head.

"Hey, two can play at this game." Nick snatched up his gun and took aim at Rachel, simultaneously relieved and disappointed that the golden moment had passed.

To Jenny's complete delight, the water fight escalated until both adults were drenched and dripping. A brief truce was called so that lunch could be consumed, then the battle resumed in the wading pool, with Jenny in the middle. Water guns gave way to beach balls and toy boats and floating plastic fish, but Jenny's favorite activity was splashing Nick. Each splash elicited a pratfall, a silly expression or some other comical reaction.

Rachel sat in the pool with the baby and laughed until she was holding her sides.

"We'd better dry Jenny off and let her take a nap, or she's going to be awfully cranky this evening," Rachel finally said.

"Okay," Nick agreed, kneeling on the grass and leaning over the edge of the pool. "I'm running out of fresh material, anyway."

Rachel laughed. "It didn't look like it. You seemed to know the moves of all Three Stooges."

Rachel stood up in the water, the T-shirt clinging to her. The wet fabric was translucent, revealing the swimsuit underneath. The damp cotton clung to her breasts, molded to her flat stomach and cupped her derriere. When she bent to lift the baby from the pool, a hard rush of arousal pulsed through him.

Forcing his eyes away, Nick busied himself plucking the toys out of the pool, but he couldn't keep from surreptitiously glancing at Rachel as she wrapped the child in a fluffy towel and carried her to the blanket on the lawn. Nick placed the dripping toys in a mesh bag and straightened as Rachel sat down, the baby on her lap, and reached for the diaper bag.

"What can I do to help?" Nick asked.

"Why don't you go get a book from Jenny's room while I change her? You can read her a story before her nap."

Nick returned and settled beside Rachel on the blanket. He could smell the herbal scent of her damp hair, the soft fragrance of perfume on her sun-warmed skin. Her thigh brushed his as she scooted over to make room for him. The warmth of her leg sent a rush of warmth through his veins.

Jenny clung to Rachel and eyed Nick warily.

"Don't worry. I'm not going to try to pick you up," he told the baby. "You can stay right there on Rachel's lap while I read." Nick held out the book. "'Once upon a time, there were three bears,'" he began.

He could almost see Jenny relax in Rachel's arms. By the time he'd finished reading the story, the baby's eyes had closed.

Rachel rose and carried the baby to the portable crib on the deck. Nick followed, watching as she gently lay Jenny in it, arranging a light blanket on top of her. Rachel turned toward him, then folded her arms across her chest, rubbing her upper arms.

"Are you cold?" he asked.

"A little." But it wasn't the temperature that was giving her goose bumps. It was the way Nick was looking at her, as if she were a piece of chocolate that he was ready to gobble up. She was intensely aware of the fact that she was scantily clad and that he'd been gazing at her in a frankly appreciative way all day.

"Well, come back out in the sunshine and warm yourself up. I intend to catch a few rays myself."

Rachel followed him to the blanket on the lawn. He sat down and patted a place beside him. It was the same place where they'd been sitting just moments ago, but without the baby, it now seemed entirely different.

Nick picked up a bottle of suntan lotion and began slathering it on his chest. The way his biceps bunched and bulged each time he bent his elbows made Rachel's mouth go dry. His stomach was as hard and flat as a marble slab, and his chest was covered with a thick mat of dark, masculine hair.

The coconut scent of the lotion filled her nostrils. She remembered smelling that scent on Nick before, one day when they'd gone hiking. She remembered inhaling it as he'd kissed her in the middle of the trail, remembered the erotic way it had crept into her senses, and remembered that afterward, she had smelled like it, too.

"Do you want some of this?"

She realized with a start that she was staring.

"You're likely to burn without it." He held out the suntan lotion.

She awkwardly accepted the bottle. "Thanks."

He shot her a teasing smile as he worked the lotion into his shoulder. "You're going to get some weird tan lines if you sunbathe with that shirt on."

"Oh. Right." Her insides quaking, Rachel nervously tugged the damp shirt over her head. She knew it provided virtually no cover, but it was unnerving all the same, undressing in front of Nick.

His gaze roamed over her, his eyes appreciative. "Wow. You look great in a swimsuit."

Rachel felt her face heat.

"Even better than I imagined."

The thought of Nick imagining her in a swimsuit both thrilled and alarmed her. Keeping her head down, she poured a glob of suntan lotion into her palm. Her hand shook as she tried to apply it to her shoulder.

"You know, it's odd that we never went swimming together out of all the times we dated."

"It's not all that odd, considering I don't swim," Rachel remarked.

Nick's brows flew high. "You don't know how?"

Oh, dear. Why had she brought the subject up? She'd

always managed to divert him to some other activity whenever he'd suggested swimming two years ago. Why couldn't she have done so now? "I know how. I just don't do it."

"Why not?"

It was embarrassing, admitting to a weakness like this. Especially in front of a man like Nick, who apparently wasn't afraid of anything. Rachel shrugged. "When I was a child, I had a really bad asthma attack in the water. I nearly drowned. And ever since, I haven't been able to bring myself to get in any water that's over my head."

"You never told me."

Rachel shrugged. "There was never any reason to." She squirted some lotion on her legs and bent over, busily rubbing it in. She could feel the heat of his gaze bearing down on her more intensely than the Arizona sun.

"What was it like, having asthma?"

"Scary," Rachel admitted. "One moment I'd be fine, and the next I'd find it next to impossible to draw a breath. The worst part was not knowing when it would happen."

"Wow, that must have been rough."

"It was. I'm glad I outgrew it."

"When was that?"

Rachel raised a shoulder. "I had my last attack at the age of twelve, but for years I lived in fear of having another one."

"Do you ever worry about it now?"

Rachel grinned, trying for a flippant air. "No. I'm too busy worrying about other things."

"Like what?"

Like the way you make my stomach flutter. Like the way I feel all hot and shivery inside every time you look at me like that. Like how delicious it feels, being here with you now, smelling your lotion-scented skin and looking at your very male, half-naked body.

"Like—like…" She searched desperately for something

trivial to say, something that wouldn't give away the direction of her thoughts. Her gaze fell on the bottle in her hand. "Like how I'm going to get this suntan lotion on my back."

Nick flashed a devastating grin. "Well, that's one worry I can take off your mind. Turn over and lie down."

Oh, dear. Out of everything she could have said, why had she come up with *that?* Now she had no choice but to comply.

Rachel stretched out and rolled onto her stomach. The blanket was soft and sun heated, and the grass underneath it made a surprisingly plush mattress. Over her shoulder, she could see Nick pour the lotion into his hands and rub his palms together. Her body tightened in anticipation of his touch.

Nick didn't fail to notice. "You're tense." His hands were large and strong, and the lotion was warm. He rubbed it on her shoulders, kneading the muscles, stroking his way down her shoulder blades. He lifted a strap of her red suit and rubbed the lotion under it, then repeated the action on the other side.

Pleasure rippled through her. He took his time, spreading the lotion slowly, languorously, deliberately—across her shoulders, down her spine, down to the deep dip at the bottom of her swimsuit, under the plunge of the armholes beside her breasts. Desire, hot and intense, coiled within her. She wasn't sure when the lotion application became something more, but she was gradually aware that it had.

His hands slid down her body, stroking, massaging, caressing, inflaming. She felt helpless to stop it. She didn't want to stop it. The hot coil inside her unwound and blossomed until it was a deep, throbbing ache.

"Rachel." She felt his breath on her neck as he whispered her name. He stretched out beside her, still working his magic with one caressing hand. She opened her eyes to find his face inches from hers. His green eyes were heavy-lidded, dark and full of desire. She was dying for him to kiss her, yearning for it with all of her soul.

He claimed her lips gently, like a slow-motion, soft-focus scene from an old romantic movie. The kiss started out light, soft, feather-gentle, then rapidly gained momentum. The next thing she knew, they were hungrily clinging to each other, struggling to close all distance between them. Nick rolled on top of her, covering her with the delicious weight of his body, pressing the hard evidence of his desire intimately against her.

It was heaven. It was home. It was as if he'd never left.

Rachel clung to him, hurtling back in time. Her heart was right back where it had been when he'd left. Once again, she was ready to give herself to him, to tell him she loved him, to promise that she would be his forever.

But Nick didn't want forever. Nick didn't want love. Nick didn't want commitment.

Nick didn't want *her*, because those things were part and parcel of who she was and what she had to give.

The realization cut through the thick, drugging fog of desire like an intrusive beam of light.

"Nick," she murmured.

His mouth slid across her cheek, heading toward her ear, toward the shivery, thrilling kisses she knew he would deliver there. She pushed against his chest. "Nick. I—we—can't."

He lifted up, then rolled onto the blanket beside her. The sudden absence of his weight, of his warmth made her want to cry. She gazed at him, her heart breaking as it had two years ago when the door had thudded closed behind him.

There was nothing to say that hadn't been said before, nothing he didn't know. She scrambled to her feet.

He caught her hand.

"I—I'd better go inside and change." Pulling her hand free, she fled toward the house.

Distance seemed to be the only effective safeguard. Time

had conferred no immunity to him. Even heartache had failed to cure her.

Distance was the only defense she had against Nick Delaney, but her job denied her that luxury.

Her job, and the sleeping baby on the back porch—a baby who was starting to pose just as big a threat to her heart.

Chapter Five

Nick glanced at Rachel as he steered his Acura into the Barrington parking lot early the next morning. She was sitting rigidly beside him, her hands neatly folded in her lap, her eyes fixed straight ahead. Conversation between them during the brief ride from his house to the office had been as stiff as Rachel's posture.

She was the very picture of professionalism. Her hair was pulled away from her face in a no-nonsense ponytail low on the nape of her neck, her white blouse was buttoned to the neck and her gray jacket hid any hint of female curves. It was hard to reconcile this all-business, buttoned-down professional with the fun-loving, water-squirting, hot-kissing woman of yesterday.

A pang of guilt shot through him. He'd been out of line, kissing her like that. He never should have touched her. Hell, he probably shouldn't have looked at her, once she peeled off her T-shirt. Just the thought of how she'd looked in that slinky red swimsuit was enough to get him hot and bothered all over again. Even more disturbing was the memory of how she'd responded.

She'd been as aroused as he was. Her lips had clung to his, and her arms had clutched at his back. He felt a fresh stirring of desire at the memory.

Hell's bells. What he needed to remember, he told himself sternly, was how she'd broken away and fled into the house. Regardless of how much she'd seemed to enjoy the kiss at the time, the fact remained that Rachel didn't want to get involved with him again any more than he wanted to get involved with her.

He'd tried to apologize to her yesterday afternoon, but Rachel had cut him off. "Look, I think we can both agree it was a mistake."

Nick had nodded uneasily. "That's why I wanted to apologize."

Rachel had dismissively waved her hand. "We just fell into an old habit, and old habits die hard."

"Old habit?" Her choice of words had irritated him. "Like biting your fingernails?"

Rachel had nodded. "You and I have a habit of responding to each other physically."

Old habit. Heck. She made it sound like they were a couple of old ballplayers trying to stop spitting in public.

"I know how you hate having what you call 'relationship discussions—'" Rachel had carved quotation marks in the air with her fingers "—so let's just agree it won't happen again."

She was right; Nick hated talking about relationships. The topic always turned to commitment, and when it did, he inevitably found himself in a no-win situation.

"So what do you say?" she'd asked.

"Fine," he'd managed.

"Good. Let's just go on as if it never happened."

But, dammit, it *wasn't* fine. It *had* happened, and he'd been able to think of little else ever since. It had evidently weighed heavily on Rachel's mind, too, judging from how she'd gone out of her way to avoid him the rest of yesterday afternoon. She'd focused all of her energy on the baby, barely bothering to give him a glance. And after they'd put Jenny to bed for the night, Rachel had promptly retired to her room and stayed there the whole evening.

His jaw clenched, Nick steered the vehicle into his personalized parking space and killed the engine.

"Well, here we are," he said unnecessarily.

Rachel turned and smiled at the baby. "Ready to come out of your car seat, Pumpkin?"

It was amazing, the way Rachel's face lit up and softened when she spoke to the baby. He remembered when she used to look at him that way. The thought sent a pang of something akin to longing coursing through him.

Put a lid on it, Delaney. Unfastening his seat belt, he hit the button on the dashboard that opened the car's trunk.

"I'll come around and get your door."

"Oh, don't bother. You have your hands full, getting Jenny's equipment out of the trunk."

Her refusal rankled. Whether she wanted to admit it or not, he was a man and she was a woman, and there were certain courtesies to be observed.

Ignoring her remark, he circled the car and jerked her door open. "No lady ever opens her own door in my car." He reached out his hand and gave her a challenging smile. "It's another of my old habits."

Rachel hesitated, then put her hand in his. Sure enough, the contact sent enough electricity racing through him to illuminate all of Phoenix. Judging from the way her hand trembled, she felt it, too. He knew it was irrational, but a burst of triumph shot through him.

He turned and opened the back door by Jenny's car seat. "That applies to even the smallest of ladies." He smiled at the baby, who was giving him a worried frown. "Don't worry, Peanut. I won't try to pick you up. I'll let Rachel do that while I get your stroller."

They made quite a spectacle, entering the building a few

minutes later. Rachel pushed Jenny in the pink floral stroller, a frilly pink diaper bag slung over the shoulder of her tailored gray suit. Nick staggered under the burden of a collapsible playpen, a mesh bag of toys, a backpack full of blankets and diapers, and a sack containing Jenny's snacks and lunch.

They made their way across the lobby to the elevators amid the curious stares of their co-workers. Nick was relieved when the elevator doors closed behind them, only to reopen in the accounting department. Here, at least, he was on his own turf.

He followed Rachel into her office, set the bags on the floor and unfolded the playpen across from her desk. He glanced at his watch, then looked up at Rachel. "I have a meeting with Rex and the executive committee in ten minutes. It's supposed to take all morning. But I'll be back here at noon to help you feed Jenny lunch."

His voice sounded tight and pressured. It was no wonder, she thought sympathetically. It was his first day in his new position, and she knew he wanted to make a good impression.

"Good luck with your new job," she said softly.

"Thanks." He gave her a warm smile, and the awkwardness between them seemed to evaporate. "I hope you have a good morning, too." Nick turned to Jenny, who was still in her stroller. He reached out his hand, as if he wanted to touch her, then evidently thought better of it and drew it back. "See you later, Peanut. Try not to give Rachel too hard a time."

Rachel drew a deep breath of relief as Nick left her office. Ever since that kiss, the strain of being alone with him had stretched her nerves to the breaking point.

She leaned over the stroller and grinned at Jenny. "It's just you and me, sweetheart. Ready to come out of there?"

She unfastened the safety belt and lifted the baby into

her arms just as Patricia and four of her other friends came traipsing into the office.

"Oh, this must be the baby you called me about!" Olivia made a beeline for Jenny, her pregnant belly preceding her into the room by about six inches. "Did you take her to Dr. Jackson? Is she all right?"

"Yes, and she's fine. Thanks for the referral."

"She's adorable!" Newly married and expecting her first child in four months, Olivia reached for the child. "Can I hold her?"

Jenny turned her face against Rachel's shoulder and immediately started to whine.

"She's very bashful with strangers," Rachel explained.

"That's right, Olivia. Don't take it personally," Patricia piped up. "The baby treated me like a fire-breathing dragon. The only person she seems to like is Rachel. She took to her like a fish to water."

"I hear the baby isn't the only one who's taken with Rachel," said Cindy slyly. A personal assistant who worked in the New Products Division, the green-eyed brunette was recently engaged to marry the vice president of her department. In fact, it was at Cindy's engagement party that Rachel had spilled the beans about Nick, confessing to her friends that she'd hoped he'd been about to propose when he'd abruptly left town two years ago.

Rachel fidgeted now, fearing she was about to regret her uncharacteristic confession.

Her fears proved to be founded. "Is it true?" Molly asked excitedly. "Is the man you wanted to marry back in town?"

Rachel cringed.

"Not only back in town, but heading up Barrington's Accounting Division," Patricia confirmed.

"And this is his baby?" Molly's hazel eyes were as large and round as dinner plates.

"It's his niece," Rachel explained. "His brother and

wife were killed in an accident, and Nick is now the child's guardian."

"Oh, how noble!" Molly exclaimed, her hands clasped to her bosom. "He sounds like a knight in shining armor!"

Rachel gave a weak grin as Cindy rolled her eyes. An advertising department copywriter, Molly could make acid rain sound romantic.

Sophia stepped forward, her hands on her hips. The blue-eyed blonde had just been named assistant to the new incoming executive vice president. "So where were you all weekend?" she demanded. "I called and called, hoping to find out if your new boss has any news about my new boss. All I got was your answering machine."

"Me, too," Patricia chimed in. "I was dying to know how things went with Nick on Friday. Where were you?"

It was pointless to try to hide the truth. "I was with Nick."

Sophia's eyes flew wide. "All weekend?"

Rachel nodded. As her friends exchanged knowing glances, she hastened to explain. "No! I mean, yes, I was with him, but…"

"Which is it? Yes or no?" Cindy demanded.

"It's not like you think," Rachel said quickly. "He called me early Saturday morning because the baby wouldn't stop crying. I thought Jenny needed to be checked by a pediatrician, so I called Olivia for a recommendation."

"That's right. She did," Olivia confirmed.

"The doctor said she's grieving the loss of her parents." Rachel briefly filled them in on the doctor's recommendations.

"So you've moved in?" Cindy asked incredulously.

"Well, yes, but just for the week. And it's purely platonic."

Rachel looked around at her friends' grinning faces and patted Jenny's back.

"It is!" she insisted.

"Right," Cindy said with a knowing wink at the other women.

"Yeah, sure," Olivia intoned wryly.

"Whatever you say," Sophia chimed in.

Patricia's eyebrows knit in worry as she looked at Rachel. "I just don't want to see you get hurt."

"I won't. There's nothing between Nick and me anymore."

Patricia arched an eyebrow. "I saw the way you two looked at each other Friday afternoon."

"It was just the surprise of seeing each other again," Rachel hedged.

"Did Nick explain why he left so suddenly?" Sophia asked.

Rachel nodded.

"And?"

"He said we were getting too involved, that it wasn't fair to me. He doesn't want to get tied down, and he knows I want marriage and family."

"Oh, that's so romantic!" Molly clasped her hands together. "He must have really cared for you."

Rachel shifted Jenny to her other shoulder. "Look, this is all ancient history. There's nothing between Nick and me now. Can we please change the subject?"

But her friends weren't ready to let it go.

"So nothing happened all weekend?" Cindy eyed her closely. "No long, lingering looks? No kisses? Nothing at all?"

To her chagrin, Rachel felt her face flame before she could form an answer.

"I knew it!" Cindy exclaimed. She perched on the edge of Rachel's desk and leaned forward. "So tell! We want to know everything."

"There's nothing to tell. Nothing's going on. I'm simply helping him out with the baby." Rachel looked at her friends challengingly, wanting desperately to convince them. "I'd do the same thing to help any of you."

Olivia placed her hand on her pregnant belly and smiled. "I'll remind you of that when Junior here arrives."

Patricia suddenly glanced at her watch. "Speaking of arriving, I've got four job applicants coming in this morning. I'd better get back to my office."

Sophia checked her wristwatch, too. "I've got to run, too. I'm supposed to take notes at the executive committee meeting."

"We'd all better get to work," Cindy said.

Amid murmured agreement, the women headed toward the door.

Sophia turned, grinned and gave Rachel a thumbs-up sign. "You go, girl."

"I've seen Nick, and I don't blame you a bit," Cindy said with a wink.

Patricia lingered behind. "Be careful, honey," she whispered.

Rachel stared glumly at the door as her friends filed out. None of them believed her. All of them were convinced something was going on.

Rachel hugged Jenny as she walked toward the playpen. It bothered her that her friends had so little faith in her ability to put the past behind her and treat Nick merely as an old friend.

But most bothersome of all were the doubts she harbored herself.

"Okay, Jenny—here it comes!" Squatting beside the stroller, Nick waved the rice cereal and mashed banana-laden baby spoon as if it were an aircraft. "Open the hangar—here comes the plane!"

Jenny stubbornly turned her head, her lips sealed as tightly as a Ziploc storage bag, her chin defiantly tucked against her pink terry-cloth bib.

Nick sighed and lowered the spoon into the bowl on his lap. "She still won't let me feed her."

"But you're making progress," Rachel reassured him. "She smiled when you walked in the door. And she's letting you get a lot closer than yesterday."

Which is more than I can say for you, Nick thought disheartenedly. Ever since that unwise kiss, Rachel had been keeping her distance as if he had terminal halitosis.

"I got your memo about the departmental staff meeting this afternoon," Rachel remarked.

Nick nodded. "We have our work cut out for us. Rex wants every property in the chain to conduct an internal audit."

"I guess he wants to make sure everything is shipshape before he turns the reins of the company over to his son."

Nick nodded. "That's what he said."

Rachel eyed him curiously. "Have you ever met Rex the Third?"

Nick shook his head. "No one in Barrington seems to have met him. I understand that he's been in Europe, getting training from the ground up with a similar company."

"My friend Sophia has been appointed his assistant. She's wondering what he's like."

"Well, she's not alone. We're all wondering about him." Nick reloaded the spoon and held it out. "Come on, Jenny girl. Let's give it one more try. Open wide!"

Jenny again stubbornly turned her head.

"It's no use." Sighing, Nick withdrew the spoon. "I'd better let you take over feeding duty." He started to rise. Just then, Jenny's tiny hand shot out and grabbed the bowl. Before he could get out of the way, she'd dumped rice cereal and mashed banana all down the crotch of his pants.

"Oh, no!" Nick moaned.

"Oh, dear!" Rachel gasped.

Jenny's cheeks puffed out in a merry laugh.

Rachel hurried forward, a napkin in her hand, then froze, the napkin suspended in midair above his groin.

"You'd better let me do that," Nick said dryly, looking down at his pants.

Rachel silently handed him the napkin, her cheeks turning scarlet.

Jenny clumsily clapped her hands and giggled merrily. Nick cocked an eyebrow in the baby's direction as he gingerly wiped himself off. "I wish I could find a way of making you smile that didn't involve spilling food all over my clothes."

He heard a noise that sounded suspiciously like a snicker. He looked up to see Rachel trying to suppress a smile, her hand over her mouth.

Nick rubbed at the enormous glob. All he seemed to be doing was spreading the slime. As he tried to wipe it up, the napkin disintegrated, adding paper fuzz to the mess.

"Do you have any water in here?" he asked.

Rachel handed him a bottle of mineral water off her desk.

"Thanks." Nick poured some on the goo, which had the approximate consistency of paste. It ran down his leg, adding a dark, wet stain to the existing mess.

Nick stifled an oath. "Great," he said in disgust. "It's my first day as vice president, I'm holding my first meeting with my staff in an hour and I look like I've just wet my britches."

Rachel burst into laughter.

"I'm glad you find this situation amusing," he said dryly.

"I can't help it," she said, struggling not to laugh. "You look like a poster boy for Depends."

In spite of the situation, Nick found himself smiling back at her. "Oh, good. That's just the image I was hoping to project."

Rachel's peals of laughter were almost worth the impending embarrassment he was about to suffer. It was funny, he mused, but she could make him feel better about nearly any situation.

"If you'll take your slacks off, I'll clean them for you in the ladies' room," she offered. "There's a hand dryer in there I can use on them."

Nick gazed ruefully at his slacks. His options were pretty limited. His own attempts to fix the dilemma were only making it worse.

"It should only take about ten minutes," Rachel added. "You can stay in here with the door closed and watch Jenny until I get back."

What the hell. His boxer shorts probably revealed less than the swim trunks he'd worn yesterday. "All right." Nick reached for his belt buckle.

Rachel abruptly turned around, her face aflame, and bent over the stroller.

"I'll put Jenny in her playpen and give her some crackers and juice. That ought to tide her over until I can get back and feed her." Rachel knew she was babbling, but she couldn't seem to help it. The sound of a zipper being undone and the soft rustle of wool made her breath come in hard, rapid puffs. Keeping her eyes averted, she settled the baby in the playpen.

"Here you go," Nick said, holding out his slacks to her

Her face hot, she reluctantly turned around, then found she couldn't suppress her laughter. The sight of Nick in black socks, a long-tailed white shirt, an impeccably knotted tie and gray boxer shorts covered with yellow happy faces was more than she could stand.

"Be sure and come back," Nick growled as he reluctantly passed her his slacks. "It would be a dirty trick to run off and leave me like this."

Rachel dangled his trousers from her hand, the belt buckle flopping against her wrist. "That's a real temptation," Rachel teased. "I've finally got you where I've always wanted you."

Nick cocked an eyebrow. "Undressed?"

She didn't know it was possible, but her face grew still hotter. "I meant completely at my mercy."

"But I've been there all along, sweetheart." Nick flashed a rakish grin. "I've been there all along."

His eyes held a dangerous glimmer. All of a sudden, the lighthearted, teasing mood shifted and changed to something more substantial, something with deep undercurrents and dark, murky depths.

"I—I'd better get to work on these before that stain starts to set," Rachel said. She abruptly left the room, taking his trousers with her.

Nick stared at the closed door behind her for a long moment after she left, wondering if she had any idea how true his remark had been.

Ten minutes later, Nick glanced at his watch for the umpteenth time. "She'll be back soon," he told the screaming baby, gently setting her back in her playpen.

Lord, he hoped he was right. The child had started wailing soon after Rachel had left the room, and showed no signs of letting up since. He'd tried all the usual remedies—holding her, singing to her, even pushing her around the tiny office in her stroller. Each new attempt to calm her only seemed to infuriate the child more.

The only thing he hadn't tried was humor. He might as well give it a shot.

"Hey, Jenny—want to play doggy?" Nick promptly got on his hands and knees, scrunched his features into a silly face and peered at her through the mesh side of the playpen.

Startled, the baby stopped crying and stared.

"Woof! Woof! Woof!" Nick stuck out his tongue and panted. Jenny smiled. Encouraged, he wagged his backside. The baby burst into giggles.

Thank heavens—he'd finally found a way to calm her.

Still on all fours, he panted and waggled his happy-face clad backside again.

A breeze on his bare thighs alerted him that the door had opened. He turned his head to see the company president staring down in shocked disbelief.

"What in bald blazes is going on here?" Rex demanded, closing the door.

Nick scrambled to his feet. The gray-haired man raked his eyes over Nick's pantless legs, then stared at him as if he'd lost his mind.

"I know this must look odd, sir, but there's a logical explanation."

"There'd better be, son. And I can't wait to hear it."

The door opened again. Nick gave a sigh of relief as Rachel walked through it. Her face drained of color at the sight of Rex.

"Mr. Barrington," she gasped.

"Excuse me, sir." Reaching around Rex, Nick snatched his trousers from Rachel's hands, then turned toward the wall and rapidly pulled them on.

When he turned back around, Rex's curious gaze flicked from him to Rachel, then back again. "Delaney, will you tell me what the devil is going on?"

"It's very simple. The baby is my niece, Jenny..."

"Yes, yes, I know all about that. Very commendable, your taking on the task of raising your brother's child."

"Well, Jenny's lunch spilled on my pants and Rachel was helping me clean them." Nick quickly filled Rex in on Jenny's adjustment problems, the doctor's advice and Rachel's assistance.

"I see." The gray-haired man thoughtfully stroked his chin. "Well, it's apparent to me that there's only one thing to do about all this."

"What's that?"

"Send you both home."

Nick's heart sank to his shoes. He'd spent years working

toward this promotion, and his first day in the new position, he was about to be suspended.

Dadblast it. Drawing a deep breath, Nick pulled himself erect and prepared to face the music. "Sir, if you feel that disciplinary action is necessary, I won't argue with you, but please leave Rachel out of it. She was only trying to help me, and she shouldn't be punished for that."

"Disciplinary action?" Rex stared at him for a moment, then slapped his thigh and gave a hearty laugh. "You've been up in that cold climate too long, son, if you think I'm going to punish a couple of employees for trying to take care of an orphaned child. I'm not talking about disciplinary action. I'm talking about taking some time off—with pay, of course—to get your family affairs straightened out. I'm sure this place can muddle along for a week or so while you two help this baby adjust."

"B-But I have a staff meeting scheduled to start planning the audit, and—"

Rex waved his hand. "All that will keep." He clapped Nick on the shoulder. "Take care of your family concerns, son, and come back to the office when they're in order." Rex turned to the door, then stopped and winked at Rachel.

"I appreciate your helpfulness, Rachel."

"My pleasure, sir."

Rex grinned. "Just make sure he keeps his pants on, you hear?"

Rachel's face turned florid.

Rex laughed heartily. "Good luck, you two. Now gather up all this stuff and take that baby home where she belongs."

With that, he walked out and closed the door behind him.

Rachel and Nick looked at each other. Nick ventured a tentative grin. "Well, you heard the man. What are we waiting for?"

Chapter Six

Rachel carried Jenny through the automatic door of the
local supermarket Wednesday afternoon. Nick followed behind, pausing to grab a shopping cart at the entrance.

Rachel could feel his eyes on her as she settled the child
in the cart's baby seat and snapped the safety belt in place
around her waist.

"She sits up well for a baby her age, doesn't she?" he
remarked.

"Yes, she does."

"It won't be long before she's crawling. She's making
all the preliminary movements—getting up on her knees,
rocking back and forth, rolling across the floor."

Rachel's eyebrows rose. "I'm surprised you know all
that."

Nick grinned. "There was a book in Jenny's things about
the development of babies. I've been reading it."

Rachel's chest filled with warmth. Nick was obviously
growing attached to the child. She'd been vaguely worried
that Nick was going to try to keep the baby at emotional
arm's length ever since he'd said he didn't want Jenny to

call him Daddy, but her concerns along that score had eased in the past few days. They'd interviewed nannies all day yesterday and again this morning, and Nick's selectiveness had impressed her. So had his attentiveness to the baby. He seemed to love nothing more than making Jenny laugh.

It was clear that Jenny was growing fond of him, too, Rachel reflected. The child smiled when he walked in the room and perked up at the sound of his voice. She reached out and grabbed at him when he played with her, let him feed her and even allowed him to change her diaper.

But she hadn't yet let him hold her. Or rather, Nick hadn't tried since the day they'd left the office.

"I'm going to wait and let her make the first move," Nick had said when Rachel had questioned him about it. His eyes had taken on a teasing light. "It's the same approach I'm using with you."

Rachel had laughed, but her heart had thudded furiously. "Don't hold your breath," she'd told him.

But that was exactly how she felt whenever she was alone with him—as if she were holding her breath, waiting for something to happen, hoping…

Hoping what? Rachel caught herself up short. She knew better than to hope for something that could never be.

Besides, Nick might be growing closer to Jenny, but he was deliberately keeping his distance from Rachel. Each night after they put Jenny to bed, Nick would excuse himself and disappear into the study to peruse the stack of files he'd brought with him when they'd left the office on Monday. He said he needed to work on developing the internal audit guidelines, but Rachel suspected he was deliberately avoiding being alone with her.

Which was fine, she told herself. They had no business being alone together. Sexual tension continued to sizzle between them, filling the air with an electrical charge that made it hard for her to keep her eyes off Nick. She'd often caught him gazing at her, too, in a way that made her blood run fast and hot.

As a matter of fact, he was doing it right now. He looked away as she met his gaze.

"I'll drive," he said, assuming the spot behind the cart. He leaned down to Jenny. "This way I can make sure we cruise down the cookie aisle." Nick's conspiratorial wink made Jenny giggle.

Yes, Nick and the baby were definitely bonding, Rachel thought, following them into the produce section. She stopped beside him next to a display of melons, where an elderly woman in a red dress was thumping a cantaloupe. The woman's wrinkled lips stretched into a smile as she spotted Jenny. "Oh, what a precious child!" She reached a frail hand out to the baby.

Jenny promptly grabbed Nick's shirt and buried her face against his chest.

Nick smiled apologetically. "She's kind of shy."

"Oh, my great-granddaughter is the same way," the woman said in a frail, vibrato voice. "Terrified of strangers, but very affectionate with family." The lady smiled again. "Your child seems affectionate, too. Why, it looks like she wants you to pick her up right now."

Nick's brows flew up in surprise. "It does?" He stared at Jenny, who was stretching her tiny arms in the air, then turned questioningly to Rachel. "Do you think so?"

His eyes were so eager and hopeful that it made Rachel's heart ache. He looked like a young boy who'd just spotted a bicycle on his front lawn on his birthday and wasn't quite sure if it was for him. A lump formed in her throat as she nodded. "Sure looks like it to me."

Nick quickly unfastened the red safety strap, then slowly, cautiously lifted the baby from the cart. Jenny clung to his neck. Smiling broadly, he awkwardly patted her back.

The old woman placed the cantaloupe in her basket and grinned at Jenny. "That's better, isn't it? No place feels as safe as Daddy's arms.'' The woman glanced at Rachel. "Except for Mommy's arms, of course.''

Rachel noticed that Nick didn't bother to correct the woman about the nature of their relationship. He was too absorbed in holding the baby against his shoulder. Rachel held her breath as the woman toddled off, afraid that Jenny would revert to form and start crying. Nick, too, seemed cautious. He stood rooted to the spot, patting the baby's back, until the child raised her head and gazed around.

"The lady's gone,'' he told her. "The coast's all clear.''

Jenny looked into his face, then stretched out a hand and touched his jaw. She abruptly pulled back her fingers, a surprised look on her face.

Nick grinned. "A little rough, huh? That's called a five o'clock shadow.''

Jenny reached out and tentatively touched his face again, then broke into a cherubic smile.

Nick's eyes filled with pleasure and pride. "Hey—I'm holding her, and she's smiling!''

Rachel nodded. "She sure seems to like it.''

Nick's smile was ear to ear, filled with unabashed delight. "What do you say, Jenny—want to hang out with me while we shop?''

Jenny's teeth gleamed as she grinned. Nick beamed just as widely. "Looks like you'd better take over as shopping cart driver,'' he said to Rachel. "I seem to have a new job—official baby carrier.''

"So I see.'' Their eyes met, and Rachel felt as if her heart was full to bursting, overflowing with emotion. It seemed an unlikely place for a miracle—an impersonal, fluorescent-lit supermarket, with Muzak humming in the background and dozens of shoppers going about their everyday errands—but Rachel knew a miracle was happening all the same. A baby had opened her arms and her uncle had opened his heart. A new family was being born.

A new family that didn't include her. Rachel blinked

back the tears that inexplicably formed in her eyes and looked down, pretending a keen interest in the melons.

She was being ridiculous, she silently scolded herself. She'd known from the beginning that her role was to help Nick form a relationship with the baby, then move out of their lives. And yet, over the past few days, she'd enjoyed playing house with Nick and Jenny. It had been a wonderful fantasy, pretending that she belonged there, pretending that she was Jenny's mother and Nick's wife.

That was the problem, she thought glumly. It had been too wonderful.

Because the truth was they weren't a family, and they weren't going to become one. Not as long as Nick thought marriage was about as pleasant as Chinese water torture.

A cold emptiness ached in her chest. She needed to face it. No matter how tender and warm and funny Nick was, no matter how longingly he looked at her, no matter how devoted he became to Jenny, he had no intention of ever getting married. And all the pretending in the world wouldn't change that fact.

"Thank you for coming, Mrs. Evans," Nick said the next afternoon, opening the front door wider. "Please come in."

Holding Jenny on her lap, Rachel watched as yet another nanny applicant sent by the child-care agency entered the living room. This one was a short, rotund woman with salt-and-pepper hair. Her lively brown eyes creased into a warm smile as she spotted the baby.

"Oh, what a little darling!"

To her credit, the woman stopped in her tracks and clasped her hands together. The other nannies had all made a beeline for Jenny, making the child cower and hide her head against Rachel's shoulder.

Nick gestured toward Rachel. "This is my friend Rachel,

who's been kind enough to help me out with Jenny. Rachel, Jenny, this is Mrs. Evans."

Mrs. Evans smiled at Rachel. "It's very nice to meet you. Is Jenny bashful with strangers?"

"Very," Nick confirmed. "She only started letting me hold her yesterday. She still prefers Rachel."

The woman's eyes grew warm. "The agency told me that the poor child had recently lost her parents."

"That's right."

"Well, it's important to be patient and affectionate, but not to overwhelm her. She needs time and space to adjust to things at her own pace."

Nick glanced at Rachel. "That's almost exactly what the pediatrician said."

Mrs. Evans smiled. "Thirty years ago, my husband and I adopted our son after his parents were killed in a boating accident. Every baby is different, of course, but I have a pretty good idea of what you and Jenny are going through. It must be a difficult adjustment for both of you."

Nick and Rachel exchanged a silent glance. All nine of the applicants they'd interviewed so far had been more than qualified, but this one was special. Even Jenny seemed to agree. Instead of averting her eyes, she was staring at Mrs. Evans with open curiosity.

Rachel sat silently as Nick asked Mrs. Evans questions about her background, her experience and her child-care philosophy. She knew it was irrational, but the more perfectly the woman responded to the questions, the further her spirits plummeted.

She was about to be phased out of Nick and Jenny's lives. It was what they'd intended all along, but it hurt all the same.

She gazed at the baby, snuggled contentedly on her lap, and tightened her embrace on the child. Jenny had completely, irrevocably stolen her heart. The thought of not being about to hold her like this made her arms ache.

She loved Jenny. Just like she loved Nick.

The thought filled her with alarm. Determined to push it from her mind, she forced her attention back to the conversation at hand.

"I'll need someone during the weekdays from seven in the morning until six or so at night," Nick was saying to Mrs. Evans. "Every now and then I'll need to go out of town, and on those occasions, Jenny's nanny will need to stay here with her for the duration of the trip. Would that be a problem for you?"

"No, not at all. I'm very flexible."

Nick glanced at Rachel. Rachel flashed what she hoped was an encouraging smile, then looked down at Jenny, wanting to hide the tears in her eyes.

"You sound ideal for the job. Could you start work on Monday?"

Mrs. Evans hesitated. "Is that the day you're going back to work?"

Nick nodded.

"If I might offer a suggestion... It will probably be easier on Jenny if you phase me in gradually."

And phase me out the same way. Rachel swallowed around a hard lump in her throat.

Nick's face grew thoughtful. "You're right. What do you suggest?"

"Well, perhaps I should come over for a few hours Saturday afternoon, then stay a while longer Sunday. That way it won't be such a shock to Jenny when she's left alone with me for the entire day on Monday."

"Sounds like a good plan." Nick turned to Rachel. "What do you think?"

Rachel swallowed hard. "I—I think Mrs. Evans is right. And that'll work out fine for me. I have to attend my friend Olivia's baby shower on Saturday, anyway."

Jenny whimpered and shifted restlessly. Rachel was glad for an excuse to leave the room. "I think Jenny's hungry.

If you two will excuse me, I'll go fix her a snack while you iron out the details.'' Carrying the baby, Rachel fled the room. Like a prisoner about to face the gallows, she had the distinct feeling that time was running out.

"Sweet dreams, sweetheart. Have a nice nap.'' Rachel leaned over the crib on Friday and kissed the baby's downy cheek, then raised the safety rail and tiptoed out of the nursery. This was the last time she'd tuck Jenny in bed for an afternoon nap, she thought sadly, pulling the door softly closed behind her.

It was all coming to an end. Tomorrow morning she'd pack her things and return home. After that, she'd only see Nick at the office, and rarely see Jenny at all.

She headed down the hall, her heart heavy. She hated to leave. The fact that the three of them had acted more and more like a real family as the week had progressed wasn't making her departure any easier. She and Nick had spent a wonderful time with the baby in the neighborhood park this morning, watching Jenny play in the sand and taking turns pushing her in a swing. Jenny had gurgled and laughed and kicked her legs, protesting only when it was time to leave.

Nick had stopped at a toy store on the way home and bought Jenny a swing of her own. He'd hung it on the back porch as soon as they'd gotten home, then pushed the child until she'd nearly fallen asleep.

He might not want to think of himself as a father, but he was turning into a wonderful, doting dad all the same. He was patient and affectionate and tender, and Rachel was finding new things to love about him every day.

Love. Oh, dear, there was that word again. She'd tried to avoid thinking about it, but the more time she spent with Nick, the more often it cropped into her thoughts.

Well, she had to figure out a way to keep it at bay. She was going to have to work with him every day, and if she didn't want to be miserable, she'd have to find a way to squelch these warm, tender feelings every time they started to emerge.

She needed to remind herself of all the reasons he was a heartbreak waiting to happen, she told herself sternly. Instead of looking for things to admire about Nick, she needed to look for flaws and faults.

She didn't have far to look. As she reached the bottom of the stairs, his voice drifted out of his study and into the hallway. "Barrington Resort on St. John, please," she heard him say.

Curious, Rachel froze and listened.

"Could you please connect me to the marina?" There was a brief pause, then he spoke again. "Yes. I want to charter a boat for a couple of scuba expeditions next month."

Scuba expeditions? Rachel could hardly believe her ears. The first thing he did after hiring a nanny was to plan a trip away from the baby?

A sense of outrage pulsed through her. He evidently couldn't wait to resume a freewheeling bachelor life-style, Rachel thought hotly. Never mind that an emotionally fragile, orphaned baby was just learning to trust him and starting to regard him as her father. Rachel had thought he'd enjoyed staying home this past week with her and Jenny, but the little stint at domesticity must have left him champing at the bit.

She waited until Nick hung up, then marched into the study. Planting her hands on her hips, she glared at him across his desk. "I've never heard of anything so selfish in my life."

Nick's eyebrows rose and his forehead creased in surprise. "What?"

"Planning to go off and leave Jenny the moment you hire a nanny so you can take a vacation."

Nick's eyes narrowed. "Who said anything about a vacation?"

"I couldn't help but overhear your conversation with the resort in St. John."

"Oh, that." Nick waved his hand dismissively. "I'm just planning the annual hotel controllers' retreat."

"I heard you setting up some scuba expeditions."

Nick's mouth curved in wry amusement. "Yes. I'm setting up several different outings for the controllers who care to stay over an extra day."

Rachel was flustered. "But—but what about Jenny?"

"She's going, too. So is Mrs. Evans. I discussed it with her yesterday after you left the room." Nick rose from his chair and circled his desk, his expression serious. "I wouldn't leave Jenny just as we're starting to bond."

Remorse poured through Rachel. "I—I'm sorry I jumped to the wrong conclusion."

"Well, I guess I can understand why you would." Stepping closer, he took her hands. "It's sort of what I did to you, isn't it?"

The pain and sadness in his gaze filled her chest with an unwanted tenderness. For a long, heart-stopping moment, they simply gazed at each other, their eyes locked, their souls talking. The air grew heavy with emotion, and for a moment, Rachel thought Nick was about to kiss her.

Then he abruptly turned and rounded his desk, placing it between them. He cleared his throat and picked up a pencil. "Jenny and Mrs. Evans and I aren't the only ones going to St. John. You're going, too."

"Me?"

Nick nodded. "I'm going to need some assistance selling the staff on the need to conduct internal audits. Think you can pull together a presentation on that?"

The question left her completely flustered. "Well, yes, but..."

"But what?"

But I hadn't counted on seeing you outside the office, after tomorrow. Rachel gazed at him, emotions battling inside of her. One part of her was delighted at being included in his plans. The other part feared it would only make it harder to create the self-protective distance she needed.

"I know it's beyond the realm of your usual job responsibilities, but it would be a good experience for you," Nick continued. "Besides, if you're looking to move up the career ladder, you'll need to start doing presentations like these sooner or later."

She had to separate her feelings for Nick from her job, she told herself sternly. Otherwise she'd never be able to work with him. This was a business issue, and she needed to base her decision about it on the basis of what was good for her career, not what was good for her heart.

She drew a deep breath. "I'll be glad to do it. Of course, I'll need a lot of information—what data you want collected, how you want the audit conducted and so on."

Nick nodded. "We'll work all that out. In fact, if you have a moment, why don't we sit down and brainstorm it now?" His smile was heart-meltingly winsome. "I've always really valued your judgment."

And she'd always valued feeling needed.

He'd always known exactly what button to push, she thought glumly, easing herself into a chair as he pulled up one beside her. She couldn't allow herself to fall for it again. Nick didn't really need her—not in the way she longed to be needed, anyway. And if she let herself imagine that he did, even for a moment, she'd end up more heartbroken than she already was.

Rachel glanced at her bedside clock late that night— 2:37 a.m. With a sigh, she pushed back the covers and climbed out of bed. She'd been lying awake for more than an hour, thinking about leaving, and growing more depressed by the minute.

Maybe a glass of milk would help put her back to sleep. Pulling on her short satin bathrobe, she tiptoed down the stairs and into the pitch-black kitchen. She groped along the wall until her fingers found the light switch.

"Oh!" she gasped.

The bright lamp over the breakfast table revealed Nick sitting there, staring out the bay window at the darkened backyard. He abruptly turned toward her, his expression as startled as she felt.

She backed toward the doorway, feeling like an intruder. "I—I didn't know you were in here," she stammered. "I'm sorry. I didn't mean to disturb you."

Nick rose, his chair screeching on the hard tile floor. "You're not disturbing me. I could use a little company."

Rachel swallowed hard. He was wearing only a pair of sweatpants. His bare chest was tanned and muscled, covered with dark, masculine curls. His hair was rumpled, and a lock of it fell over his forehead. He looked like he'd just rolled out of bed.

She'd never seen a sexier sight in her life.

She was embarrassed to realize she was staring. She was even more embarrassed to realize that Nick was staring back.

She glanced down. Oh, dear—no wonder. Her robe hung open, exposing the sheer pink camisole and tap pants she'd worn to bed. Clutching her robe protectively around her, she reached for the sash and cinched it tight.

She searched her mind for something—anything—to say to relieve the awkwardness she felt. "What were you doing, sitting here in the dark?"

"Thinking. What about you? What are you doing awake?"

"I couldn't sleep. I thought a glass of milk might help." She headed to the refrigerator and drew out the milk carton. "Want some?"

"Sure."

Rachel selected two glasses from the cabinet, splashed milk into them, then carried them to the table. "What were you thinking about?" she asked, lowering herself into a chair.

Nick sat down next to her. "Nothing."

"Looked like a pretty serious nothing," Rachel observed.

Nick ran a hand down his jaw and sighed. "The truth is, I was thinking about Ben."

Rachel's heart flooded with sympathy. "It must be hard, losing a brother."

"The hardest part is how unfair it all is." His voice held a sad, bitter edge she'd never heard before. "Ben's whole life was unfair."

"What do you mean?" Rachel asked softly.

"I've done just about all the things that Nick and I used to talk about doing when we were kids. I've gone skiing and scuba diving and hang-gliding. I've gone sailing and spelunking and on safari." Nick looked down at the table-top, tracing the wood grain with his finger. "But Ben never got to do any of those things. He was too busy shouldering the responsibilities I ran off and abandoned when I left the farm."

"'Abandoned'—that's a pretty harsh word," Rachel said softly. "Is that what you're feeling? Like you abandoned Ben?"

Nick blew out a ragged breath. "It's what I did, isn't it?"

"No," she said softly. "It's not." She reached out and placed her hand on his. He looked up, his mouth tight. "You went to college. You didn't commit some kind of crime."

His mouth curled sardonically. "You'd have thought it was. My father told me I'd let four generations of relatives down by not carrying on their family tradition."

"I don't believe that, and I don't think you do, either.

You never would have left if you honestly did." Rachel tightened her grip on his hand. "You know what I think? I think you set a great example for your brother. You found the courage to follow your own dreams, and by doing that, you encouraged him to do the same thing."

Nick stared at the tabletop. "It didn't work that way. He stayed behind, trying to fill the role I was supposed to fill. Do you have any idea how guilty that makes me feel?" Pulling his hand free, Nick stood and paced the kitchen. "I tried to make it up to him. I offered to pay his way through college, but he wouldn't leave the farm. I offered to get him a job with Barrington. He could have worked at any of our resorts, anywhere in the world. He wouldn't leave Oklahoma. Then, when he got married, I gave him and Nancy an all-expense-paid honeymoon to Hawaii as a wedding gift, and do you know what he did? He cut the trip short because he was worried about an early freeze at the farm."

"He sounds to me like a man who loved what he was doing," Rachel said softly. "Maybe he *was* following his dream."

Nick leaned against the kitchen cabinet and gazed at her. "I wish I could believe that."

"People change," Rachel said gently. "And when they do, sometimes the things they want out of life change, too." She hesitated. "Do you know what I wanted to be when I was in high school?"

"A preschool teacher. And you let your parents talk you out of it, just like Ben let my father control his life."

His words stung, but Rachel didn't let him derail her from the point she was determined to make. "I meant before that," she said quietly. "Believe it or not, I wanted to be a rock musician."

Nick looked up, his eyes incredulous.

Rachel gave a wry smile. "I know, I know—it's ridiculous. I'm shy, I'm conservative, I don't like crowds, I don't play a musical instrument and I can't carry a tune in a bucket. In the whole history of the world, there's never been anyone less suited to a career. It's funny to look back on now, but I used to sit around for hours, dreaming about how great it would be and talking about it with my girl-friends.''

"I don't understand how that applies to Ben."

"Don't you see? It was an alter-ego fantasy—a way of mentally trying on a life-style I'd never have, a life-style that was fun to think about, but would have made me miserable if it ever happened. Maybe that's what all the talk of travel and adventure was to your brother. Maybe Ben's real definition of happiness was something completely different.'' She rested her hand on his arm and waited until he looked up at her. "Maybe having a wife and a child and working the farm were what really made him happy.'' Rachel hesitated. "Maybe he was afraid to tell you that because he thought it wouldn't sound exciting enough.''

She couldn't read Nick's expression, but he at least seemed to be listening. Encouraged, Rachel forged ahead. "You showed Ben that anything is possible if you just have the courage to pursue it. I wish I'd had someone set an example like that for me. I've lived my whole life feeling like the lion in *The Wizard of Oz*, looking for a way to acquire some courage.''

"Really?'' Nick's brow knit together, his gaze acute and penetrating. "What are you afraid of?''

"Oh, lots of things. Making a fool of myself, mostly. Failure. Swimming. Asthma attacks.''

"I thought you'd outgrown the asthma.''

Rachel looked down at her fingers. "It ruled my life for a lot of years, and it left me with a lot of emotional scars. It made my parents overprotective, which left me overly cautious and afraid to take risks. Sometimes I feel like a timid little mouse.''

Nick reached out and took her hands. "But you're not timid now."

The touch of his fingers sent a electrical charge racing through her. "Oh, yes, I am."

"I don't see you that way."

And that's one of the key reasons I love you, Rachel thought suddenly. *When I'm with you, I'm most like the person I've always wanted to be.*

Chances were, she'd never find anyone who made her feel that way again. The realization sent an empty ache through her chest.

"I don't see you that way at all," Nick repeated.

"That's probably because I don't feel so timid when I'm with you."

His fingers softly rubbed the back of her hands. "I'm glad," he said softly.

Rachel's heart pounded furiously. She knew she should look away, knew she should do something to end the escalating sexual tension, but something deep inside her refused to do so. "I still don't have the courage to go for the things I really want," she murmured.

"Sure you do. What do you want?"

Nick's eyes held hers, as tightly as his fingers held her hands. His gaze was compelling, making something she never knew she had rise and well up inside her.

"Come on, tell me," he urged. "What do you want more than anything else in the world?"

Only their hands were touching, but he was close enough that she could feel his body heat.

"You mean right now?" Her voice came out uncharacteristically husky and low.

"Right this very second."

His eyes were dark green pools, both tempting and dangerous, luring her, daring her to tell him. She gazed into them, drew a deep breath, then dove headfirst. "For you to kiss me."

The words were feather soft, barely even a whisper, but they hit Nick with the force of a jackhammer. In a heartbeat, he closed the distance between them and gathered her into his arms.

He was flooded with sensation. The cool satin of her robe, the heat of her body underneath. Her breasts, full and warm, flattening against his chest. The sweet weight of her arms winding around his neck. The soft, familiar scent of her perfume. The tremulous flutter of her lips beneath his, the salty taste of her mouth as the kiss deepened and grew.

There was nothing timid, nothing hesitant about her now. She kissed him with a hunger and an urgency that matched his own. She ran her fingers through his hair, pulling his head closer. Her lips moved and moaned beneath his mouth, opening for him, urging him on.

"Rachel." As if from a great distance, he heard himself murmur her name.

"Nick," she breathed. "I want…"

The rest of her words were lost in the kiss. The sash of her robe slipped to the floor, and one of her long, silky legs wrapped around him. The feel of it inflamed him. Before he knew what he was doing, he'd picked her up and lifted her to the kitchen counter. The neckline of her camisole hung provocatively low, barely covering the pebbled tips of her breasts. He bent his head and kissed the valley of her cleavage, just above the delicate medallion of lace.

He was like a man dying of thirst in the desert. He wanted to drink her in, to drown himself in her, to come up for air, then dive down all over again. Dozens of buried memories fluttered through his mind like butterflies bursting from their cocoons. The velvet softness of her mouth the first time he kissed her on Squaw Mountain. The way her hair gleamed with copper highlights the day they'd hiked in the desert. The way her eyelashes fell in soft shadows against her cheek in the lamplight of her doorway when she used to close her eyes for a good-night kiss.

A low moan escaped her throat. Her head was thrown back, and her hair spilled down her spine as she leaned back. Nick kissed his way up her neck, his lips lingering at her throbbing pulse point, then sliding upward to again claim her mouth.

His hands drifted up her back to her shoulders, where they toyed with the thin straps of her gown. He kissed her ear, reveling in the responsive way goose bumps formed on her flesh. She wound her legs around his waist, pressing herself intimately against him.

"Rachel..." His blood roared in his ears. The need to remove all barriers between them grew hot and urgent. He claimed her mouth in a shattering kiss, his fingers easing the straps off her shoulder. And then...

Rachel suddenly went stiff and rigid. Her hands froze on his back.

"What's wrong?" Nick whispered.

"Jenny's crying."

Sure enough, the familiar wail of the baby wafted faintly down the stairs.

Rachel pulled her hands from his back and drew away. "We need to go see what she needs." Tugging her camisole back in place, she slid off the counter. Nick turned to follow her and was treated to the heart-stopping sight of her satin-clad derriere bending to pick up her bathrobe.

Like a man in a trance, he followed her up the stairs and into the nursery. He watched as Rachel picked up the baby.

"What's the matter, sweetheart?" she crooned to the child. "Did you have a bad dream?"

Nick didn't know about the baby's dreams, but she sure had a bad sense of timing.

Or maybe it was an excellent one, he thought ruefully. He had no business—no business at all—getting romantically involved with Rachel again. He knew that intellectually, but he seemed to have recurrent amnesia on that point. Every time she got near enough to touch, logic and reason flew out the window.

Chapter Seven

Rachel's five friends pounced on her the moment she walked into the private party room at the Mexicali Café the following afternoon for Olivia's baby shower luncheon.

"What's happening with you and Nick?" Molly asked eagerly.

"We want to know all about it," Sophia demanded.

"That's right," Cindy agreed, taking Rachel's pink-and-blue-wrapped gift and adding it to the pile of baby-themed presents stacked on the center of the round table where the rest of the women were seated. She pulled out a chair and motioned for Rachel to sit down. "The whole office knows Rex sent you and Nick home to care for the baby. You've been there with him all week, and you haven't called any of us. So what's going on?"

Molly leaned forward on the table, her straight blond hair swinging against her face. "Yeah! We want details—lots of details."

"Tell us everything!" said Olivia eagerly, her hands folded over her pregnant belly.

Rachel momentarily considered fleeing the room. Instead, she hesitantly lowered herself into the chair. "There—there's nothing to tell," she said evasively. She pretended a keen interest in the pink and blue balloons tied to a giant cardboard stork in the corner. "Say, these decorations look great!"

Cindy rolled her green eyes. "We're not going to be diverted that easily. Come on, Rachel—you don't really expect us to believe nothing's going on, do you?"

"Yeah! This is the man you wanted to marry two years ago!" Molly said.

"The guy you've been carrying a torch for ever since," piped up Sophia.

"The guy that no other man can measure up to," Patricia added.

Was it that obvious? Rachel had no idea that her friends knew so clearly how she felt. Until this week with Nick, she hadn't really known herself.

Well, maybe she'd known, but she'd been in denial. After last night's kiss, though, there was no way she could avoid facing the truth. She was still as crazy about Nick as she'd been when he'd left.

Crazier, she silently amended. Now that she'd seen his tenderness with Jenny, she was more in love with him than ever.

Love. The word made her swallow hard. It was painful to admit, but it was true. *Love* was the only word that came close to describing what she felt for Nick. Unfortunately he was just as determined as ever to keep from loving her back.

But now that he'd opened up about his family, she could at least understand why. Nick thought that loving someone meant giving up his own dreams. In Nick's mind, love meant grim obligations, oppressive responsibilities and surrendering his hard-won control of his own life. No wonder he wanted no part of it.

And he didn't. He'd told her as much as soon as she'd rocked Jenny back to sleep last night.

"I'm sorry about what happened downstairs."

"It wasn't your fault. It was—"

Nick had raised his hand, cutting her off. "I know, I know," he'd said curtly, his mouth grim. "An old habit."

That hadn't been what Rachel had been about to say at all. But he hadn't given her a chance to explain. He'd simply turned and marched into the master bedroom, closing the door behind him.

Olivia's voice jerked her back to the moment. "Don't keep us in suspense, Rachel. What's going on with you and Nick?"

"Come on, guys." Rachel tried to smile persuasively. "I thought this was supposed to be a baby shower, not an inquisition into my love life."

"Aha!" Olivia raised a finger in the air and triumphantly looked around at her friends. "She admits she's got a love life!"

Rachel sighed. "I swear, Olivia, ever since you started studying for your bar exam, you've been acting like Perry Mason."

Olivia grinned mischievously. "All you have to do is tell us the truth, the whole truth and nothing but the truth, and we'll let you off the witness stand." She again folded her hands on top of her tummy. "Let's start by establishing the facts. Has he kissed you?"

Rachel hesitated. She could tell by the way her friends were grinning that the heat flooding her face had already given her away. "Yes," she reluctantly admitted.

The women smiled at one another knowingly.

"But that doesn't mean anything's going to come of it," Rachel insisted.

"So you claim," said Olivia.

"Where there's smoke, there's fire," Cindy chimed in.

"Trust me on this one." Propping her elbows on the

table, Rachel rested her head in her palms and sighed. "Nick had some things in his childhood that made him dead set against marriage."

"But he obviously has strong feelings for you," Sophia pointed out.

"That doesn't mean he'll change his mind about marriage," Rachel said.

Patricia wrinkled her brow. "What are you going to do? It's going to be awfully hard on you, working with him under the circumstances." Patricia shook her head ruefully. "Believe me, I know."

Rachel smiled sympathetically at her friend. Patricia had fallen madly in love with her own boss, Sam, the moment she'd started working for him six months ago. Rachel knew how Patricia had suffered as she'd watched her boss make plans to marry another woman.

Rachel exhaled a long, dejected sigh. "I've given some thought to asking for a transfer."

"You can't!"

"We need you!"

"You're going to be a bridesmaid at my wedding!" Cindy said.

Rachel smiled wanly. "I don't really want to leave, but I don't know what else to do."

"It's simple," Molly piped up.

"It is?"

Molly's fine hair bobbed as she nodded. "All you've got to do is find a way to change his mind about marriage."

"Oh, is *that* all?" Rachel said dryly.

"Well, look around the table," Sophia chimed in. "Cindy, Olivia and Molly all thought their love lives were hopeless, and they found a way to work things out. If you work at it hard enough, I'm sure you can, too." Sophia's lips curved into a sly smile. "I know *I* intend to. I've been making plans ever since I was named assistant to the new executive vice president. As soon as Rex Barrington the

Third steps foot into the office, I'm going to cast a line and start reeling him in.''

Rachel stared at her friend. ''But you haven't even met him yet!''

''It doesn't matter,'' Sophia asserted. She pushed a blond curl behind her ear and gazed at Rachel earnestly. ''I want a big family, and I want to be a stay-at-home mom while my kids are little. I promised myself that my children would never grow up poor like I did, so I need a husband who can provide financial security. The Third can fill the bill.''

''What about Mike from the mailroom?'' Rachel asked.

''What about him?'' Sophia's eyes grew wary.

''I've seen him hanging around your office quite a bit.''

To Rachel's amazement, Sophia uncharacteristically blushed. The other women didn't fail to notice.

''I knew it!'' Molly exclaimed. ''You've got a thing for him!''

''I do not,'' Sophia said defensively. ''I want more out of life than a mailman can offer. He just happens to be interesting and very nice, that's all.''

''Not to mention to-die-for handsome,'' Cindy dryly added.

''Well, he can't offer financial security. I've made up my mind that I'm going to marry the Third, and that's all there is to it.''

Rachel leaned back in her chair and sighed. ''Well, I don't care about Nick's financial status. I only care about his ability to commit.''

''I know what you mean,'' Patricia commiserated. ''That's how I feel about Sam.'' She looked shyly around at her friends. ''And I've decided to do something about it, too.''

The note of determination in her voice made Rachel look at her in surprise. ''What do you mean?''

''I found out yesterday that Sam isn't getting married after all. So I'm going to strike while the iron is hot.''

"How?" Sophia asked.

Patricia lowered her voice. "I'm going to try to seduce him."

The women all began to excitedly chatter at once.

Cindy's voice carried above the rest. "What are you going to do, Patricia?"

"I don't know yet. I'm still working out the details. But I'm going to seize the moment." Patricia's jaw firmed into a determined angle. "I'm not going to let the one thing I want more than anything in the world pass me by without making an effort to go for it." Patricia reached out and patted Rachel's hand. "And I think you should do the same thing. It's plain to see you're in love with Nick."

Rachel gazed around the table at her friends. If only she were as bold as Sophia or as daring as Patricia, she thought wistfully. She'd give anything if what Patricia was suggesting were possible. "What do you think I should do?"

"Figure out what he finds most irresistible, then dangle it in front of him like a carrot on a stick."

At that moment, the side door to the room burst open and two waiters wearing black pants and embroidered vests marched in, bearing steaming trays of enchiladas, chili con queso and tacos.

"Speaking of irresistible, here comes our lunch." Olivia rubbed her hands together. "Thank heavens. The baby and I are starved!"

"You and that baby are always starved," teased Cindy.

Rachel sat back as the conversation turned to Olivia's pregnant eating habits, letting the lighthearted banter swirl around her. Was there any way she could put Patricia's advice into action?

Simple seduction wouldn't work. She and Nick shared a powerful physical chemistry, but that wasn't enough to overcome Nick's fear of commitment. If they got physically close without resolving the underlying issue, it would only make the situation worse.

She had to come up with another answer.

What did Nick find irresistible?

"A challenge," Rachel murmured aloud an hour and a half later.

"Well, sure it is, but having a baby is also one of life's most rewarding experiences," Patricia remarked, holding the restaurant door open for Rachel and Sophia as they toted out the giant cardboard stork. The three women had lingered behind the others to take down the decorations and settle the bill.

"I'm not talking about having a baby. I'm talking about what Nick finds irresistible." Rachel squinted at the bright sunshine as she and Sophia stepped outdoors. "It's a challenge. That's why he goes for all those adventure sports. It's even why he's so good at his job. He's always setting a new challenge for himself, always trying to improve."

"Terrific," Patricia said enthusiastically. "Then all you've got to do is make yourself seem like the biggest challenge he's ever faced."

"That's all, huh?" Rachel eyed her skeptically. "And exactly how am I supposed to do that?"

"You could make yourself seem unattainable," Sophia suggested.

"Sounds great, but there's one little flaw with your logic. He's not interested in attaining me."

"He is, too. I've seen the way he looks at you. He's just fighting the urge." Patricia pointed to her car on the far side of the parking lot. "We need to haul Mr. Stork that way."

Holding the cardboard stork's beak while Sophia held the tail, Rachel stepped off the sidewalk and followed Patricia, who carried a large bouquet of pink and blue balloons.

"If he sees other men interested in you, I guarantee his self-control will snap," Patricia added.

Rachel gave a wry grin. "In case you haven't noticed, I'm not exactly fighting off male admirers."

"You would be if you seemed more approachable."

Rachel shook her head. "I'm not the flirtatious type."

"Who said anything about flirting? All you have to do is act friendly and interested." Patricia unlocked her trunk. "The rest will take care of itself. It never hurts to show your assets to their best advantage, either."

"What are you talking about?" Rachel placed the bird inside.

Patricia closed the trunk, then thoughtfully looked her up and down. "I'd say your best features are your legs, your hair and your smile. What do you think, Sophia?"

"I agree completely," Sophia said.

Rachel felt her face color. She was out of her mind for offering them the least bit of encouragement, but she couldn't seem to help herself. "Just what would you two suggest I do?"

"Well, you could start by hemming your skirts a little higher," Patricia suggested.

"And start wearing your hair loose," Sophia chimed in. "Let's see what you look like without those barrettes."

Hesitantly, Rachel reached up and unfastened them. Sophia nodded encouragingly. "Oh, that's much better! It would look great parted on the side."

"But this is the really important thing—you need to make more eye contact with men and start smiling more. Be more outgoing. With everyone except Nick, that is."

Sophia leaned against the side of the car and nodded her concurrence. "When you're with Nick, you need to act a little vague, a little distant, as if you're preoccupied. You want him to think you have something—or someone—else on your mind."

"That's right. Be friendly, but unavailable," Patricia advised. "If he asks you out, tell him you're busy."

"Absolutely," Sophia agreed. "Men are always attracted

to women who don't seem to need them. Make him wonder what's going on.''

Patricia snapped her fingers. "The company picnic is in two weeks. That would be the perfect opportunity to let Nick see you having fun, surrounded by male admirers, living a full and interesting life without him.''

Rachel sighed. "I hate to burst your bubble, but in order for Nick to think my life was full and interesting, I'd have to be bailing out of an airplane at ten thousand feet.''

"Oh, that's a wonderful idea!" Sophia exclaimed.

Rachel stared at her friend incredulously. "You want me to take up *skydiving?*''

Sophia grinned. "Well, it doesn't have to be that extreme, but taking up an exciting sport—something he'd never expect you to do—is a great idea.''

Patricia nodded enthusiastically. "It would make him see you in a whole new light. Especially if he had no idea you were learning how to do it, and you just sprung it on him.''

Sophia's head bobbed in agreement. "That's right. If he starts seeing you as a sports partner, maybe you won't seem so threatening as a life partner.''

Rachel had to admit it made some sense. Nick had been deprived of play in his childhood, and he needed to make up for lost time. If he started to view her as a partner in adventure, the idea of marriage might seem a lot less frightening.

And she knew exactly which sport would be most effective.

"Scuba diving,'' she muttered under her breath. She looked up, surprised to find that she'd actually said it aloud.

Patricia's eyebrows rose. "I thought you were afraid to swim.''

"I am. That's why scuba would be so perfect.'' She couldn't believe she was actually contemplating this, but the thought made her heart pound with excitement. "He's got a financial directors' meeting scheduled in St. John in six weeks, and I happen to know he's got a scuba expedition scheduled.''

"Oh, wow," Sophia said excitedly. "You could take lessons, get certified and just show up at the boat. You'd knock him off his feet!"

"But what about your fear of swimming?" Patricia repeated.

Rachel hesitated. All of her life she'd played it safe. She'd avoided risks, she'd used caution, she'd lived by the adage, "When In Doubt, Don't." Her life had been ruled by fear—both the fears of her overprotective parents and the fears of her own timid nature. And every time she'd given in to it, it had gained a stronger hold on her.

Fear had limited her. It boxed her in. It had clipped her wings, imprisoning her like a bird in a cage.

She'd always avoided risks, but suddenly doing nothing seemed the biggest risk of all. If she did nothing, she could never become the kind of woman she'd always longed to be—a woman with strength and confidence, a woman unafraid to pursue her dreams, a woman with the courage to face and conquer the things that held her back.

The kind of woman who could win Nick's heart.

He needed a woman who would encourage his zest for life, who wouldn't hold him back or restrain him or weigh him down as his father had done. He needed a woman who would show him that love could be freeing and joyful and fun. A woman with whom forever didn't sound like a life sentence, but not nearly long enough.

She wanted to be that woman. She wanted it more than she wanted anything in the world—badly enough to face her deepest, darkest fear.

"Aren't you afraid of deep water?" Patricia asked again.

She hadn't been back in the water since that awful day she'd nearly drowned. She wasn't sure how she'd react to being in water over her head again.

But she was already in over her head, she thought ruefully. She was in love with Nick and Jenny.

She looked at her friends and drew a deep breath, her chest filling with resolve as it filled with air. "You know what I'm even more afraid of? I'm more afraid of looking back on my life when I'm old and gray, and regretting the things I was too scared to try." Her mouth firmed into a determined line. "There's a pool at my apartment complex. When I get home, I'm going to start in the shallow end and gradually work my way deeper. Before this day is over, I'm going to be swimming in the deep end."

"Way to go!" Smiling broadly, Patricia patted her on the back. "Want some company? It's a beautiful day for a swim."

"I'd better come, too," Sophia chimed in. "I know CPR."

They all laughed. Rachel wrapped her arms companionably around both of her friends' shoulders, a lump forming in her throat. "You guys are the best. I really appreciate the moral support."

Patricia smiled at her fondly. "That's what friends are for."

"Rex really knows how to throw a party, doesn't he?"

Nick looked up as a pot-bellied accountant named Henry strolled by his picnic blanket, wearing a Hawaiian shirt and baggy shorts.

"Sure does," Nick agreed. "These company picnics get better every year."

"No kidding," Henry agreed. "Lake Pleasant is the best site yet. But the best part is the chow. I'm heading back to the main pavilion for more barbecue, then I intend to hit the dessert station." Henry motioned to the covered shelter twenty feet behind him where the caterers were serving watermelon slices, giant cookies and other treats on tables covered with long red-and-white-checked tablecloths. "Want me to bring you anything?"

Nick shook his head. "No, thanks. I ate my fill. I'll just kick back and watch the volleyball game while Jenny here sleeps."

The man nodded and ambled off. Nick glanced down at the baby, who was peacefully napping beside him, then turned his attention back to the game.

But it wasn't the game that held his interest. It was Rachel playing it.

Nick watched her spike the ball over the net and let out a whoop of victory. Something was different about her. He couldn't exactly put his finger on it, but something about her had changed in the past two weeks.

Part of it was her appearance, he mused. She was doing something different with her hair. Instead of restraining it with barrettes, she'd started letting it float around her shoulders in a way that made it hard for him to take his eyes off her.

Her clothes seemed different, too. He'd never noticed before how her tailored business suits showed off her rounded calves and slender thighs. Whenever he looked at Rachel's legs, he couldn't help but remember how they'd felt wrapped around him that night in the kitchen. Just the thought was enough to send a surge of arousal pulsing through him.

It was happening right now. Of course, the way Rachel looked in those sexy red shorts wasn't helping the situation. When had she started wearing such bright, eye-catching colors? Rachel used to always dress in understated tones.

But her clothing wasn't the only thing that was brighter lately, he reflected. So was her personality. She'd become a lot more outgoing and sociable. Lately she'd been smiling and chatting with everyone she saw.

Especially with men. Nick's mouth tightened into a scowl. Rachel had never been the flirtatious type, and he couldn't exactly call her flirtatious now. After all, she seemed just as friendly and outgoing with women as with men. But her demeanor had changed, and all of a sudden, men were flocking around her like bees to a field of clover. She seemed more open, more confident, more accessible somehow.

More accessible to everyone except him, he thought with a scowl. Where he was concerned, she seemed to have grown oddly distant. She never had time for chitchat and friendly banter anymore. She was pleasant, but professional.

In fact, she was treating him exactly as he'd hoped to treat her. So why did it bother him so intensely? Probably because she was so darn good at it, he thought darkly. Try as he might, he couldn't forget all that they'd been to each other.

Rachel, however, seemed to have put their romance completely behind her. Her only personal interest in him centered around Jenny.

When it came to the baby, she couldn't get enough details. She wanted to know the results of Jenny's follow-up visit with the pediatrician, how she was adjusting to Mrs. Evans, what foods she was eating and what new things she'd learned. Rachel's face had lit up when he'd told her Jenny had begun to crawl. Seeing Rachel smile like that had made Nick feel all warm and fuzzy inside, and he'd longed to make her smile that way again.

He'd asked her out to lunch. After all, he'd figured, just because they'd agreed to keep their relationship platonic didn't mean they couldn't still be friends. She'd turned him down, saying she had other plans. He'd countered by asking her to dinner. She'd smiled regretfully, telling him she was busy that evening, too.

Rachel never used to be too busy to go to dinner with him, he'd silently groused. ''What's got you so occupied lately?'' he'd asked point-blank.

"Oh, lots of things," she'd said vaguely. She'd glanced at her watch and made an excuse to hurry away.

Nick had felt a pang of something that felt suspiciously like jealousy. He'd called her house that evening to see if she were actually home, and hung up when he'd gotten her answering machine. Unable to contain his curiosity, he'd driven by Rachel's apartment on his way home from an errand to see if her car was parked in her spot. It wasn't. Only the fact that it was nearly Jenny's bedtime and he hadn't yet given her a bath kept him from sitting there and waiting to see what time Rachel came home.

Not that it really mattered, he told himself. He had no claim on Rachel. He was just curious, that was all. It wasn't like her to be so secretive. As an old friend, it was only natural that he'd be concerned about her well-being.

Nick watched her score a point for her team. He'd assumed he'd finally get a chance to spend some time with her at the picnic, but when he and Jenny had arrived, she'd been surrounded by a group of athletic-looking junior executives from the marketing department. He'd breathed a sigh of relief when she'd immediately rushed over to him, but his relief was short-lived.

All of her attention had been focused on Jenny. The baby had squealed with delight as Rachel had lifted her from his arms. Rachel had toted the baby around to all her friends, letting them ooh and ahh over her, while Nick had tagged along like a third wheel.

Rachel had accompanied him through the buffet line and joined him on his picnic blanket, but only, he suspected, so she could feed Jenny lunch and admire the baby's newly acquired crawling skills. Afterward, Rachel had rocked the baby to sleep. As soon as Jenny was settled for a nap, Rachel had sprung up and sprinted away to join the volleyball match.

He turned his attention back to the game, which was growing increasingly boisterous. A muscle-bound man with a thick shock of blond hair caught Rachel around the waist and picked her up to congratulate her for a particularly successful spike.

A nerve ticked in Nick's jaw. He glanced over at Jenny. The baby was sound asleep. She usually took a two-hour midday nap. There was no reason he couldn't join the game and keep an eye on her from a distance.

Doing his best to look casual, Nick sauntered over to the volleyball net.

"Who's watching Jenny?" Rachel asked.

Dadblast it. Couldn't Rachel think of him in any terms except as Jenny's guardian? He was a man, for Pete's sake—a man whom she'd kissed. And he intended to make sure she didn't forget it.

"She's asleep." He pointed to the blanket in the shade, less than thirty feet away. "We can keep an eye on her from here."

He turned to the muscle-bound creep who was lingering beside Rachel, his hand still on her waist. "Why don't we organize a real game? The accounting department against all comers."

He tossed a challenging look at the two men on the other side of the net. Glancing at each other, the three men shrugged, then nodded. "Sure."

Nick quickly gathered four more staff members, while the young men rounded up three more of their buddies.

When the teams were assembled, it was a far from even match. The players on the opposing team were all built like Olympic shot put contenders. Nick's team consisted of two out-of-shape middle managers, a junior accountant with an arm in a sling, Rachel and himself.

Well, that was just fine, Nick thought hotly. If Rachel went for the brawny, athletic type, well, then, he'd show her brawny and athletic. He'd single-handedly carry his team to victory. He couldn't wait to beat the barbecue sauce out of these biceps-bound Lotharios.

It was going pretty well, Nick thought smugly an hour later. Rachel had turned out to be a surprisingly adept player, and he'd managed to cover for the rest of his team. A large crowd, including Rex and his assistant, Mildred, had gathered to watch. They were halfway through the fifth game, the teams tied two and two. Nick crouched in anticipation of returning a serve when Rachel suddenly asked, "Where's Jenny?"

Nick jerked his head toward the blanket, then froze. Dear God. The blanket was empty.

He felt the blood drain from his face. The volleyball sailed right by him unheeded. Nick turned to the crowd. "Does anyone have my baby?"

The spectators looked at each other blankly. Nick pointed to the blanket. "She was sleeping right there. She's nearly eight months old. She has curly blond hair and she's wearing a bright pink playsuit."

A murmur rippled through the crowd.

Nick's heart leapt to his throat. His stomach felt ill, his skin cold and clammy. If anything had happened to Jenny, he couldn't live with himself.

"She probably woke up and crawled away," Rachel said. "She's just learned to crawl."

Nick quickly surveyed the surroundings. The blanket was bounded by a stand of trees on one side, the volleyball court on another, the dessert picnic pavilion in front and a long slope of grass leading to the shore of Lake Pleasant behind.

"We'd better check the lake," someone said.

The lake. Nick felt as if the bottom had just dropped out of his world. He gazed at Rachel and saw that she looked as horror-struck as he felt.

"Oh, no. You know how she loves the water," he muttered. "You don't suppose..."

"It's—it's too far for her to have crawled," Rachel reassured him. "It's at least a hundred feet away."

"How long has she been missing?" someone asked.

A fresh shot of guilt stabbed through Nick. He'd gotten so absorbed in showing off for Rachel that time had gotten away from him. "I don't know. Five—ten—maybe even fifteen minutes."

"Come on, everybody," Rex called. "Let's start looking for her."

"I'm going to start at the shore," Nick said grimly.

"I'll come with you." Rex turned to his assistant. "Mildred, organize a group to search the trees and behind the pavilion."

"I think we should call the police first," Mildred said softly. "Just in case."

Nick's heart seemed to stop in his chest. "Just in case of what?"

The older woman placed a reassuring hand on Nick's arm. "I just think we should notify the authorities so they can help us look, that's all."

But Nick knew what she was thinking. *In case the baby was injured. Or kidnapped. Or drowned.*

Dear Lord, how could he have let this happen? He'd gotten all caught up in impressing Rachel, that was how. Guilt, hot and anguished, poured through him.

"Use the phone in my car, Mildred," Rex said.

Nick turned to the crowd of employees. "Half of you come with me. We'll divide up once we get to the shore so we can cover more ground."

Rachel placed a hand on his arm. "I'll search around here. I'm certain she's nearby."

Nick nodded. Rachel could tell by his tense expression that he feared the worst. She'd never seen his face so ashen or his eyes so grim. Her heart turned over as she watched him stride off toward the lakefront, followed by Rex, Mike the mailman, Sophia, Olivia and her husband, and half a dozen other employees.

"Come on, Rachel," Patricia urged gently. "Let's start looking. If she crawled away, she couldn't have gone far."

"Jenny! Jenny!"

Rachel stopped under a mesquite tree, her chest filling with despair. The entire staff of Barrington's corporate headquarters had been searching for the child for ten full minutes. With each passing second, the likelihood of finding the baby unharmed decreased. Most of the searchers were now focusing on the waterfront, but Rachel and Patricia continued to scour the area closest to where the baby had last been seen.

"We've been over this ground before," Patricia said. "Don't you think we should look someplace else?"

"She's got to be around here somewhere," Rachel said firmly. "A baby that size can't crawl very far."

Patricia's brow creased with worry. "Maybe she didn't crawl away, Rachel," she said softly. "Maybe somebody took her."

Rachel's heart lurched in her chest. She wasn't ready to face that possibility. Not yet. She refused to give up hope.

"Let's give it one more try. Maybe we've just overlooked her." Rachel dropped to her knees in the grass near the picnic pavilion where the caterers had set out the desserts. "I'm going to go over the ground the way Jenny would. It's the method Nick and I used when we baby-proofed his house."

"Jenny! Jenny!" she called. She suddenly stopped and glanced up at Patricia. "Did you hear something?"

"Just the other searchers on the other side of the picnic shelter."

"I thought I heard a rustling sound." Still on her knees, Rachel turned to the right and spotted a watermelon-pink object on the ground, half-hidden by a red-and-white-checked tablecloth. She was ready to discount it as a slice of melon when, suddenly, it moved.

"Jenny!" She jumped to her feet, her heart flooding with joy. Sure enough, there was the baby, calmly munching on an abandoned slice of watermelon.

Rachel swooped her into her arms. The baby grinned broadly, tightly clutching the watermelon slice.

"Oh, Jenny, I'm so glad to find you!" Rachel cradled the child against her chest. "I'm so glad, so glad!"

Patricia cupped her hands around her mouth. "We found her! We found her!" she yelled.

Within seconds, a crowd had materialized. But out of the sea of faces, Rachel saw only one.

Nick—plowing his way through the throng, his mouth taut and hard, his eyes dark and undershadowed with worry. Oh, dear heavens—he didn't yet know that Jenny was all right.

Rachel lifted the baby high. "Nick! She's fine!"

His face was transfigured the moment he caught sight of Jenny. The hard furrow in his brow dissolved, his eyes lit with joy and his lips curved into an enormous smile.

The crowd cleared a path to let him through. And the next thing Rachel knew, he was embracing both her and Jenny in an enormous bear hug.

Rachel was vaguely aware that tears were coursing down her cheeks. Jenny laughed. And Nick clung to them both as if he'd never let them go.

He finally relaxed his hold enough for Rachel to shift the baby into his arms. He crushed the child to his chest, as if he were afraid she'd vaporize before his very eyes. "You're all right, Jenny. You're really all right." He gazed at Rachel gratefully. "Where did you find her?"

"In a place so obvious we all overlooked it—under a table." Rachel smiled. "She seems to have developed a taste for watermelon."

Grinning, Nick glanced down at Jenny, who was busily smearing watermelon all over his white polo shirt. He looked back at Rachel, his heart in his eyes. "I don't know how to thank you. I was so afraid—"

His words broke off, but he didn't need to continue. "I know," Rachel whispered.

And she did. In his eyes she could see all the words he couldn't say. At that moment, their minds seemed in perfect sync. She knew exactly what he was thinking, exactly what he was feeling. Their hearts seemed to beat as one.

The spell was abruptly shattered by Rex, who pounded Nick on the back. "Looks like this little lady really likes to mess up your clothes. Both times I've seen her, she's managed to cover you with some kind of food." Rex shook a playful finger at the baby. "Don't you know your dad is mighty particular about his clothes?"

"I don't care if she ruins everything I own," Nick said. "She's okay, and that's all that matters."

Grinning, Rex nodded companionably. "My son pulled a similar disappearing act when he was a year old. I know what you must be feeling. It's something every parent seems to go through at least once."

"Well, I guarantee it won't happen again. I don't intend to let my daughter out of my sight until she's at least eighteen."

Rex laughed again. "That's when she'll need watching the most, son." He slapped Nick's back again, then turned to the crowd. "Okay, everybody—thanks for your help. The baby's just fine, so let's get on with the party!"

Rachel gazed at Nick as the crowd dispersed, her throat thick with emotion. "You called her your daughter," she finally said.

"Well, I reckon that's what she is."

The lump in Rachel's throat made it hard to speak. "So, are you going to let her call you Daddy?"

"If that's what she decides to call me, I'll be more than honored."

For a man who didn't think he was capable of loving anyone, Nick had become awfully attached to Jenny, Rachel mused. Her heard swelled with hope.

He might not call it love, but Rachel knew love when she saw it. If Nick could open his heart to a child, maybe, just maybe, he could open his heart to her, as well.

Chapter Eight

The following Friday, Nick sat at his desk staring at the report in front of him. It was hard to focus on its contents because he couldn't get his mind off the woman who had prepared it.

Rachel had been driving him crazy ever since the company picnic last week. They'd spent the rest of the afternoon playing with the baby together, and it had been like old times, only better. He'd felt the same sense of connection, the same easy rapport, the same sizzle of attraction they'd always shared. Having Jenny around had somehow just intensified the sense of rightness and intimacy between them.

When the picnic had broken up, he'd invited Rachel to dinner.

"Oh, I can't. I've got plans." She glanced at her watch, then rose from the blanket. "As a matter of fact, I'd better get going."

What the devil was she suddenly doing with her evenings? He was dying to know. Was she seeing someone? And if so, who?

He was pretty sure it wasn't anyone who worked at Barrington. He'd watched her like a hawk all day Saturday, and although several young studs had hovered around her, she hadn't treated any of them any differently from the others.

No, it had to be someone she'd met elsewhere. Where could she have met him, and what the hell was he like?

Not that it was any of his business. Rachel's personal life was her own affair.

Affair. The thought made him loosen his collar. Judging from the heated way she'd kissed him in his kitchen two weeks ago, she was ripe for romance. He didn't want her getting involved with some no-good playboy who would break her heart.

Exhaling a harsh breath, Nick rapidly scanned the report, then picked it up and headed to Rachel's office.

Through the doorway, he saw her frowning at her computer screen. He rapped on the doorjamb, then sauntered in. "I just looked over your report. Good work."

Rachel glanced up and flushed with pleasure. "Thanks."

Nick perched on the edge of her desk. "I haven't seen much of you lately."

Rachel toyed with a pencil. "That report kept me pretty busy."

"In the evenings, too?" Nick prompted.

"No, I was able to do it here in the office."

Drats. He was going to have to take a more direct approach. "So what have you been up to lately? In the evenings, I mean."

"Oh, this and that." Nick could swear she deliberately averted her gaze. "What about you?"

"Not much."

"How's Jenny?"

"Great. Growing like a weed. Mrs. Evans told me this morning that she'd nearly outgrown all of her clothes."

Nick grinned. "I knew I'd been having more trouble than usual getting her dressed, and now I know why."

He was gratified to see her smile. "Guess you'll have to hit the mall on Saturday," she remarked.

Inspiration struck. "I suppose so, but I don't know the first thing about babies' clothing. I could really use some help."

He waited, hoping she'd take the hint. When she didn't, he leaned toward her. "Would you come with me? You'd be doing Jenny a real favor."

"Okay." Rachel paused. "But I have to be home by six."

"Why?"

Rachel looked away again. "I, uh, have plans for the evening."

There it was again—those confounded, mysterious plans. Nick frowned. "You're awfully busy in the evenings all of a sudden. Care to tell me what you're up to?"

To Nick's consternation, Rachel's face colored. "Not particularly." Her smile looked suspiciously self-conscious. "You'll find out soon enough."

Holy cow. Was she about to turn up engaged?

The thought made him feel as if his heart were being squeezed in a vise. How was he going to deal with it if Rachel became seriously involved with someone else?

Jealousy, cold and hard, gripped his gut. He had no right to be jealous, he reasoned with himself. He wasn't the right man for her. He'd told her as much. She needed a husband and family, and he wasn't in the market for that.

But what if she'd found someone who was? The thought made it hard for him to draw a breath.

Struggling to hide the sudden, heavy ache in his chest, he tried to make a joke. "Let me guess. You're planning a bank heist and I'll soon be reading about it in the papers."

Rachel laughed, but still didn't elaborate.

Well, that was fine, Nick thought grimly. It was none of

his business. If she was seriously seeing someone, he wasn't any too sure he wanted to know about it anyway.

He rapped the top of her desk with his knuckles, then hoisted himself to his feet and forced a smile. "Okay, then. Jenny and I will pick you up at ten in the morning, and we'll have you home before you turn into a pumpkin."

"I'm not sure why we brought this stroller along," Nick remarked as he navigated the empty buggy through the crowded aisle of the department store the next day. "Jenny hasn't left your arms since we got out of the car."

Rachel smiled at the chubby-cheeked baby who was busily peering over her shoulder. "She loves to be held, doesn't she?"

"Especially by you." Nick reached out and rubbed the nape of her neck as he tossed her a sexy smile. "Not that I can blame her."

Rachel's heart did a little flip at the feel of Nick's fingers on her skin. Nick had been flirting with her all morning. In fact, the way he kept pumping her for information about how she was spending her evenings sounded positively possessive.

She turned her head and planted a kiss on Jenny's cheek, wanting to hide her smile. Patricia's advice about letting Nick think he had some competition was right on target. He'd evidently jumped to the conclusion that she was dating someone else, and apparently it was bothering him considerably.

Well, good. Let him be bothered. He'd find out soon enough that she'd been spending her time taking scuba diving lessons. A little jealousy might be just the thing to make him realize how much he really cared.

For he *did* care, Rachel thought firmly. She was convinced of it. The problem wasn't his attitude toward her. The problem was his attitude toward marriage.

A display of lacy teddies caught her eye as they strolled

past the lingerie department. Her lips curved into a mischievous grin. Maybe it was time to turn up the heat a little.

Before she could lose her nerve, she stopped and fingered a sheer, peach-colored teddy hanging from a padded satin hanger. "Oh, look at this," Rachel remarked. "Isn't it beautiful?"

Nick's Adam's apple bobbed as he stared at the skimpy number. "Uh, sure. But when would you wear a thing like that?"

"Oh, just about any time." Struggling not to smile, Rachel lowered Jenny into the stroller, fastened the strap around the child's round little belly, then turned her attention back to the skimpy garment.

Nick's eyes narrowed, and she could practically see the wheels spinning in his head. "I don't get it. Do you wear it all by itself, or do you wear it under your clothes?"

"Oh, either."

Nick frowned suspiciously. "Under what kind of clothes?"

This was working better than she'd ever imagined. Rachel shrugged casually. "Any kind. Evening clothes, work clothes, date clothes. Even jeans."

She saw him cast an appraising gaze at the jeans and T-shirt she was wearing now and watched his throat move convulsively. Lifting the teddy from the clothes hanger, she held it speculatively in front of her and viewed herself in a mirror. In the reflection she saw Nick running a finger around his neck as though his collar was too tight, even though he was wearing an open-necked shirt.

"What do you think?" she asked.

"I think you're about to give me a heart attack," Nick growled.

Rachel laughed.

He wasn't kidding, Nick thought darkly. When she'd

held that thing up like that, it was all too easy to picture her wearing it.

He swallowed hard as Rachel moved on to a display of bikini panties. She picked up a pair of black ones so sheer and scant, he was surprised they weren't sold in a brown paper wrapper.

Dear Lord. The thought of Rachel wearing that speck of lace made it difficult to walk erect. Were these the kinds of things she routinely wore under her clothes, or was she picking out something for a special occasion? Neither thought was at all reassuring.

He drew a breath of relief when Rachel finally paid for the garments and the clerk placed them in a dark green shopping bag.

Rachel smiled at him cheerfully. "I need to get a few things at the cosmetics counter. Do you mind making another stop before we head to the baby department?"

"No. Not at all." Anything to get out of the lingerie department. Pushing Jenny in the stroller, he followed Rachel to the perfume counter. "I want to find a new scent," she said, picking up a glass bottle and delicately sniffing the contents.

"What for? I've always liked the way you smell."

She flashed him a brilliant smile. "Well, I think it's time for a change. I'm ready for something a little bolder. Something that makes more of a statement." She picked up an amber-colored bottle. "Here's one I've been wanting to try. *Lioness.*"

Nick gazed at the label. "'Guaranteed to bring out the animal in your man,'" he read.

Rachel took it from him and spritzed her neck. "What do you think?" She stood on tiptoe and bent her head, offering him a whiff. Nick took a cautious sniff.

"It's okay," he muttered.

"Hmm. Let's try this one."

"Mating Call," he read. "'Wear this and he'll get the

message.''' Good grief—what kind of message was she trying to send? More importantly, to whom? A spasm of jealousy ripped through him.

Rachel sprayed the other side of her neck and leaned toward him.

"I—I don't know," he said noncommittally.

"Well, what about this?"

"*Frenzy.* 'It'll drive him into one.'" Good gravy—didn't she know she didn't need a perfume to do that? She'd been doing it to him for years.

"Why the sudden interest in changing your perfume?" Nick asked, in what he hoped was a casual tone.

"Just feeling adventurous, that's all." Rachel sprayed her wrist and sniffed it delicately. "Mmm. I like this one." She held her hand out to him, then offered Jenny a whiff. The child grinned widely.

"Jenny likes it. That seals the deal. Let me get one other item, and then I'll be ready to go."

Nick reluctantly followed Rachel across the aisle, pushing Jenny's stroller.

"I'd like to look at your lipsticks," Rachel told a heavily made-up, middle-aged woman behind the counter. "I understand you have a new kissproof kind."

Kissproof lipstick! Just who the heck did she plan on kissing? Nick scowled as the woman nodded and pulled out a tray of samples.

"That's right," the salesclerk said. "It's guaranteed to stay on no matter what."

Rachel pointed to a delicate coral. "That's a nice shade. Could I try it, please?"

The saleslady expertly swabbed a sample onto a cotton-tipped stick and passed it to Rachel. Peering in the mirror on the countertop, Rachel carefully applied it to her lips.

She turned to Nick. "What do you think?"

He thought her lips looked irresistible under any condition. The lipstick, however, accented the shape of her mouth, calling attention to the little vee in the middle of her upper lip and the bee-stung swell in the center of the lower one.

But he wasn't about to tell her that. The last thing he wanted to do was help her look even more attractive to the mystery man she was evidently dating. Nick shrugged indifferently. "It's not too bad, I guess."

"It's guaranteed not to come off during a kiss," the saleslady prompted. Her ruby lips curled into a coy smile. "Perhaps your husband here would help you test it."

"Oh, he's not my husband."

"Your boyfriend, then."

"He's not my boyfriend," Rachel said.

A wave of jealousy, dark as smoke, curled through Nick's belly.

The woman batted her false lashes. "Well, maybe he can help you test it anyway."

Rachel glanced at him tentatively. The next thing Nick knew, he'd wrapped his arms around her waist, pulled her against his chest and pressed his lips to hers.

If she wanted to test that blasted lipstick, by damn, he'd give her a test worth remembering. While she was at it, she could test his kissing technique and see how it measured up to Mr. Mystery Date's.

Winding his arms more tightly around her, he bent her backward and laid siege to her mouth. She murmured in surprise, then gave a soft moan and melted in his arms.

All thoughts of testing lipstick and teaching Rachel a lesson evaporated in the sweet heat of that kiss. She parted her lips, and Nick was suddenly drowning in soft, hot sensation. The exotic scent of the freshly sprayed perfumes tantalized his nostrils, but what inflamed him to a passion almost beyond redemption was the underlying, subtle, familiar scent of Rachel.

It didn't take perfume or lipstick or lingerie to turn him on. It only took Rachel. The feel of her, the sight of her, the sound of her, the taste of her—heck, just the *thought* of her was enough to send him over the edge. There had never been another woman who made him feel like this, who set all his senses to roaring and keening, who could make him lose all sense of propriety and decorum and reason.

Reason. The thought pulled him back to semiconsciousness. He opened his eyes to see the salesclerk staring at him in fascination. He slowly straightened, pulling a limp-limbed Rachel upright with him.

He looked around to see shoppers gawking in the aisle. "Is this some kind of product demonstration?" asked a pudgy blonde with bulbous blue eyes.

The saleslady nodded. "They're testing out a new lipstick."

Nick drew away and dropped his arms. Rachel gazed up at him, glassy-eyed.

Dammit, he thought darkly. He wanted to drag her back in his arms and finish what they'd started. He wanted to crush her to his chest and never let her go. He wanted to tell her how much she meant to him, to beg her to never leave.

But he didn't believe in happily ever after. He believed in burnout and boredom and the need to be free.

So why did she make him think about things he'd never thought he'd wanted—things that were light and bright and shiny, things like white picket fences and wedding rings and baby smiles? Things that were normally associated with marriage.

He realized he was scowling at her. "Well?" he demanded.

"Well...what?" Her voice was low and breathless, her expression dazed and stunned.

"Did it pass the test?"

"The test," she echoed vaguely. "Oh—the lipstick!" She turned to the salesclerk, her face flushed, her expression flustered. "I—I guess I'll take one."

"Give me one, too," the blonde shopper piped up. "I've been looking all my life for something that would deliver results like that."

Desperate to distract himself from the raw emotions pulsing through him, Nick bent down, unstrapped Jenny from the stroller and lifted her into his arms as Rachel paid for her purchase.

The transaction completed, the saleslady started to gather up the lipstick samples. "Oh, dear—one lipstick has fallen out. Do you see it on that side of the counter?"

While Rachel tucked her wallet in her purse, Nick looked down at the floor, then shook his head.

"Uh-oh." The saleslady gazed at him, her expression alarmed and contrite.

"Uh-oh, what?"

"The missing lipstick. It must have fallen into the baby stroller."

Nick peered into the empty stroller seat. "I don't see it in there."

"Not in there. On you."

Nick glanced down. His shirt was covered with brilliant red smears. Jenny grinned, brandishing the tube in her chubby hand.

"Great. Just great." With a heavy sigh, he pried the lipstick away from Jenny's fingers, handed it to the clerk, then settled the baby back in the stroller. Straightening, he surveyed the damage to his blue-and-white shirt. "I look like a victim from a *Friday the 13th* movie."

The grin on Rachel's face told him she was trying hard to keep from laughing. "The lipstick is guaranteed to be kissproof, not babyproof. Looks like our next stop needs to be the men's clothing department."

Either that or someplace where he could have his head examined, Nick thought darkly. Why on earth had he ever thought that kissing Rachel would be a good idea?

Jenny might be a hazard to his clothes, but Rachel posed

a far more serious hazard to his mind. Not to mention to his heart.

The phone was ringing as Rachel unlocked her apartment door at ten o'clock that evening. Dropping her bag of scuba gear inside the entrance, she hurried to the living room and answered it.

"Rachel. I'm glad you're home."

Rachel grinned into the receiver, a little thrill chasing up her arm. *Nick.* He'd made several pointed remarks about her plans for the evening during their shopping expedition earlier in the day, and now he was evidently calling to see if she'd made it home.

If she'd had any idea he was so susceptible to jealousy, she would have tried this two years ago.

"I hope I'm not interrupting anything," Nick continued.

Rachel placed a hand over the receiver, afraid she might laugh out loud. She drew a deep breath and forced her voice to a carefully modulated tone, deliberately sidestepping his question.

"Is anything the matter?"

"Well, yes. It's Jenny."

The worried note in Nick's voice sent a rush of alarm coursing through her. "What's wrong?"

"I think she has a fever. She seems really warm. She was crying earlier, but now she just seems kind of listless. I bought one of those ear-type thermometers last week, but she won't let me put it in her ear. In fact, she keeps pulling at her ears as if they bother her."

"Ear infections are pretty common in babies. Have you called the pediatrician?"

"Yes. The nurse who handles the night calls told me to take Jenny's temperature and call her back."

"Do you have a regular thermometer?"

"No."

"I'll bring one over."

"Thanks, Rachel." The relief in his voice was almost palpable. "I really appreciate this. I would have called Mrs. Evans, but she's gone to Tucson to visit their daughter for the weekend." He hesitated a moment. "I hope I'm not ruining your evening."

Ruining it? No, you're making it. There was no place on earth Rachel would rather be than with Nick and Jenny, but given Nick's aversion to commitment, she didn't dare tell him that.

"I'll get there as soon as I can," she told him.

Hanging up the phone, she quickly tossed a few things into an overnight bag and headed to her car.

When she arrived at Nick's house half an hour later, he opened the door before she could even knock. He'd evidently been waiting by the window, Jenny in his arms, watching for her. The anxious look on his face touched her heart.

"How's Jenny?" she asked.

"See for yourself."

The baby whimpered and reached out her arms to Rachel. Placing her purse and a white plastic shopping bag on the hall table, Rachel took the child from Nick, murmuring soft endearments.

"She does feel warm." Rachel settled the baby in her arms and looked down at her worriedly. The child's cheeks were vivid pink, but the rest of her face seemed unnaturally pale. Her usually bright eyes looked glazed and listless. Rachel stroked the child's downy blond hair. "Hello there, sweetie. You're not feeling very well, are you?"

The baby snuggled against Rachel's shoulder and whimpered.

Rachel nodded toward the white bag on the table. "I stopped at an all-night drugstore and picked up a thermometer. Let's go in the living room and take her temperature."

The way the color drained from Nick's face made Rachel

give him a reassuring smile. "We'll put the thermometer under her arm."

Nick let out a sigh of relief and picked up the bag. "Glad to hear it."

Rachel led the way to the beige sofa. Nick rummaged through the bag, pulled out the thermometer and extricated it from its packaging. Rachel shook it down, then gently unfastened the back of the child's pink-and-white one-piece sleeper and placed the thermometer under Jenny's arm.

"That wasn't anywhere near as bad as I thought it was going to be," Nick remarked.

Rachel smiled as she held the thermometer in place. "When did Jenny get sick?"

"She started getting fussy after we dropped you off. At first I thought she was just unhappy that you'd left. She always hates to see you go, you know."

The information made Rachel's throat thicken. She tightened her arms around the baby.

"But she just kept getting worse. She wouldn't eat dinner, she didn't want a bottle and she started pulling on her ears. Then she started shivering during her bath."

Rachel pulled the thermometer out from under the baby's arm and turned it carefully. "One hundred and three," she announced.

"Wow. That's awfully high, isn't it?"

"It's pretty high," Rachel agreed. "But babies tend to run high temperatures."

"I'd better call the nurse back and see what she recommends we do." Nick crossed the room and dialed the pediatrician's number. After a brief conversation with the nurse, he turned back to Rachel.

"She said we need to give her some baby acetaminophen and ibuprofen."

"I picked up some of both at the drugstore. They're in the bag."

Nick shook his head in amazement. "What are you, a former Girl Scout? You're always prepared."

Rachel grinned back. "What else did the nurse say?"

"She wants us to take Jenny to the doctor's office at nine in the morning."

Rachel raised her eyebrows in surprise. "The office is open on Sundays?"

Nick nodded. "Only for an hour."

"Well, thank heavens she doesn't have to wait until Monday," Rachel said.

"The nurse said we need to keep an eye on Jenny's fever tonight. If it goes over one hundred and four, we'll need to put her in tepid bathwater and try to cool her off."

We. The word hung in the air. The way Nick so naturally included her in his plans to care for Jenny sent a surge of warmth racing through Rachel's veins.

He, too, seemed to notice his odd choice of words. He shoved his hands in his pockets and looked away. "I, uh, don't mean I expect you to stay."

Rachel hugged Jenny to her chest. "I'd like to. I brought an overnight bag just in case."

She thought she saw a flicker of relief cross his eyes. "Good. Jenny will feel better with you around." The brief look he cast her made her heart jump like a jackrabbit. "I will, too."

Rachel gazed at the alarm clock at her bedside. Three o'clock. She and Nick had agreed to take turns checking Jenny every two hours and she'd set her bedside alarm accordingly, but so far she hadn't needed it. Just being in the same house with Nick was enough to keep her fully awake.

Tossing back the covers, she grabbed her thin cotton robe and padded down the hall to the nursery, only to discover Nick standing over the baby's crib, wearing only a pair of pajama bottoms.

She self-consciously folded her arms over her chest, her thoughts flying back to the last time they'd found themselves awake in the middle of the night, clad only in their nightclothes. "I—I didn't expect to find you up."

"I couldn't sleep."

Rachel nodded. "How is she?"

Nick frowned. "I don't know. I think she's hot. And her breathing sounds kind of fast and shallow."

Stepping beside Nick, Rachel reached over the crib railing and felt the baby's forehead. "You're right. I'll get the thermometer."

Rachel returned to the nursery to find Nick in the rocking chair, holding the baby against his bare chest. "She doesn't look good," Nick said, his brow wrinkled with worry. "She seems kind of limp and glassy-eyed."

"Fever will do that to a baby," Rachel said. Gently unfastening Jenny's sleeper, Rachel tucked the thermometer under the baby's arm. "She's due for another dose of Tylenol. I'll go get it while you take her temperature."

Rachel hurried to the bathroom, measured out the dosage in a medicine dropper, then returned and gave it to the listless baby. Two minutes later, her heart sank as she read the number on the thermometer. "One hundred and four and three-tenths."

Nick's eyes darkened and a nerve flexed in his jaw. "We'd better get her in the bathtub, then."

Rachel nodded. "I'll go draw the water."

Nick carried in the sick child, and together they gently removed her pajamas. "She's limp as a rag doll," Rachel said worriedly.

Nick nodded, his forehead furrowing. "I don't think she can sit up in the water by herself. I'd better get in with her."

"O-Okay. I'll wait outside."

"Please stay." He looked at her, his eyes pleading. "I

intend to keep my pants on, if that's what you're worried about.''

Rachel felt her face heat. She turned away, busying herself with a towel, wanting to hide the fact that she had, in fact, been concerned about that very thing.

She nodded, self-consciously clearing her throat. "I'll hold Jenny while you climb in."

Nick carefully passed the infant to Rachel. The feel of the hot child, limp and helpless in her arms, made her heart ache with worry.

Nick stepped into the shallow water and settled himself in the tub, his long legs bent high. He reached out his arms for Jenny.

"Okay. Hand her over."

Leaning forward, Rachel carefully passed the child to Nick.

Jenny's weak, mewling whimpers as she slid into the water were far fainter than her usual hearty cries. Her blond curls and milky skin stood in vivid contrast to the dark, springy hair on Nick's tanned chest. "It's okay, sweetheart," he murmured softly. "Daddy's right here with you."

Rachel's heart swelled in her chest until she thought it might burst. She'd never loved him more than she did at this moment.

She'd never loved anyone the way she loved Nick. And she was suddenly sure, with a soul-deep certainty, that she'd never love a man this way again. He was the one, the only one, who could ever touch her so profoundly.

And she loved Jenny, too. Kneeling beside the tub, Rachel picked up a washcloth and gently sponged the child's face and neck, her throat thick with emotion.

She loved being here with them both, loved feeling like a family, loved sharing their lives in good times and bad.

Maybe especially in bad times. Because that was when she was needed the most.

The problem was, Nick didn't want to need anyone, didn't want to depend on anyone except himself. He'd spent his childhood chafing under the restrictive rules of his father, and he was determined to never let anyone control his life again. He saw need as a weakness, commitment as a loss of control.

What he didn't see yet was the joy of being needed, the sweetness of a life that is shared. But he was starting to discover it with Jenny.

Rachel swallowed hard around the lump in her throat.

"How long do you think we need to stay in here?" Nick asked. "Jenny is shivering."

"A little while longer," Rachel said. "Let's try distracting her."

Nick picked up the toy rubber duck perched on the side of the tub and tried to interest her in it, but the baby just continued her pathetic crying.

"Hey, Jenny," Nick crooned softly. "We're going to get you all well, then guess what? In a few weeks, we're going to the beach. You'll love it there. You can crawl in the sand and pick up shells. It'll be warm and sunshiny, and the water will be cool and blue. I'll hold you up in the water and you can ride the waves. It'll be great."

The baby continued to whimper. Nick sighed. "It's no use. I don't have the soothing effect on her that you do. Would you try singing to her?"

"Sure. She loves 'The Itsy Bitsy Spider.'"

Rachel lifted her voice in the familiar tune and was gratified when Jenny turned to listen. Rachel sang the entire song, complete with hand gestures, all the way through three times.

"The water's starting to get uncomfortably cold," Nick remarked.

"Then it's probably time to get out."

Rachel grabbed a towel off the towel bar and reached for the child. Nick passed Jenny to her, then climbed to his feet. The way his dripping pajama pants clung to his thighs made Rachel's mouth go dry.

Averting her gaze, Rachel wrapped the baby in the towel. "I'll get her dressed while you dry off and change," she said.

"Okay."

Nick joined them in the nursery a few minutes later, clad in a T-shirt and dry sweatpants. He found Jenny dressed in fresh jammies, sitting in Rachel's lap in the rocking chair. "Her fever's down two degrees," Rachel announced.

A rush of relief pulsed through Nick. "Thank heavens."

They gave her a bottle of juice, then took turns reading stories. Thirty minutes later, Jenny was fast asleep in Rachel's arms. Moving carefully to keep from waking the child, Rachel took the child's temperature one last time. "The medicine's taken effect," she whispered. "Her temperature's under a hundred."

"Can we put her back to bed?"

Rachel nodded. Rising slowly, she carefully carried the baby to the crib and gently set her on the mattress. Jenny moved, but didn't awaken. Rachel carefully tucked a light blanket around the baby as Nick stood beside her and watched.

He reached out his hand and stroked the baby's soft cheek. His heart swelled with an emotion he'd never known. "Good night, sweetheart," he whispered.

He followed Rachel into the hall and down to the darkened sitting area. Moonlight filtered through the window, filling the room with a mellow glow. "Whew!" he said softly.

Their eyes met, and she nodded. "You can say that again."

Nick gazed at her, his heart full of an odd, sweet emotion, ambrosial and fragrant as night jasmine. "Thanks for your help. I don't know what I would have done without you."

"You were wonderful." She looked at him, her eyes warm. "You're a terrific father."

Nick blew out a sigh and rubbed the back of his neck. "I was so worried. She looked so pathetic—so sick and small and limp...."

"I know."

"I'm really glad you were here with me."

Her eyes shone softly in the moonlight. "I'm glad I was, too."

His heart felt hot and tight, ablaze with gratitude and relief and something he couldn't quite name. It seemed the most natural thing in the world to pull her into his arms. And once he had, the next natural thing was to kiss her.

He knew it was a mistake the moment his mouth met hers. Her lips were warm and silky and urgent, and so was her body under the thin cotton of her robe. He heard the catch of her breath, and felt her heart thunder against his chest.

Or maybe it was his own; he was holding her so close, he could scarcely tell where he ended and Rachel began. He pulled her even closer, one hand around her waist, the other in her hair, his fingers sifting through the silky strands, inhaling the sweet, subtle woman scent that was hers and hers alone.

She overloaded his senses, like a warm night in the tropics. She was everything that he could imagine ever wanting. And dear Lord, how he wanted her—all of her, the whole of her, every secret, sacred part of her.

"Nick," she breathed against his cheek, her breath warm and damp. "Nick..."

The breathless, urgent way she moved against him spoke more eloquently than any words she could have uttered. Her robe fell open, and the hard pearl buttons of her short pink nightgown bit enticingly into his chest.

Desire, thick and hot, throbbed through him. The master bedroom was mere feet away. Bending abruptly, he swept her off her feet, one hand under her knees, the other under her back, and carried her to the large, draped bed.

She pulled him down with her as he eased her onto the rumpled covers. His mouth slid from her lips to the slender column of her neck, then down to the pulse point in her throat. He worked the tiny pearl buttons of her nightgown free, pushed aside the pale fabric, and claimed a dimpled nipple. The small bud hardened and flowered in his mouth as she moaned with pleasure.

"Nick," she murmured. The blood thundered through his brain as she moved beneath him, raising a roaring din in his soul.

Rachel was in his bed, hot and hungry and eager. He could have her as he'd always wanted her. He could brand her soul, he could mark her heart, he could claim her as his own. And if he did, he would no longer be tormented by the thought of her with another man, because he knew that if Rachel loved him in this way, she would love him in every way. If she gave him her heart, she would give it for keeps.

Which was the very reason he had to stop. The thought forced its way through his passion-fogged brain like an intrusive beam of light.

He had to stop. Rachel was a forever kind of woman, and he didn't believe in forever.

He pulled back. She reached out and tried to draw him close again, but he stiffened his arms, holding himself away. He pushed up and sat on the edge of the bed. "This is a mistake," he grunted.

"No, it's not. It's what we both want."

She wasn't making it easy. It took every ounce of his willpower to haul himself to his feet. "Well, it's a bad idea. If we take things any further, we'll regret it in the morning."

"I won't." Her voice was just as soft and sure as it had been two years ago. It wrenched the depths of his heart.

He risked a glance at her, then wished he hadn't. Her face was luminous in the moonlight, her eyes shining like sapphires. Her unbuttoned gown fell open as she rose from the bed, exposing the deep valley between her breasts.

He turned away, knowing all of his resistance would evaporate if she touched him again. "Well, I would," he growled. "Now go back to your room and get some sleep."

"Is that what you're going to do?"

"Hell, no. I'm going to take a cold shower. And I better not find you still in my bed when I get out."

He strode through the bathroom door, yanked it shut behind him, then, for good measure, he turned the lock. He didn't really think Rachel would follow him in here—but then, he never would have thought Rachel would have kissed him so heatedly in public, or acted like such a seductress in private. He was discovering all sorts of new and disturbing facets to her personality.

He couldn't help but wonder who else was making the same discoveries. He hadn't questioned her about her whereabouts this evening because he hadn't been sure he could deal with the answer.

Heaving a huge sigh, he stripped off his clothes, stepped into the shower and turned the cold water on full blast.

Chapter Nine

When Rachel walked into the Barrington break room Monday afternoon, it was empty except for a table occupied by Olivia and Patricia.

"Olivia just told me you spent most of the weekend with Nick," Patricia said excitedly. "What happened?"

Rachel had been asking herself the same thing. Inserting several jangling coins in the soda machine, Rachel punched her selection, picked up the can and headed to the table. Pulling the tab, she sat down between Olivia and Patricia and sighed. "Well, Jenny was sick and the nanny was out of town. So I spent Saturday night at Nick's house helping him care for her, then went with them to the doctor's office the next morning. Mrs. Evans came back Sunday afternoon and agreed to spend the night, so I went home."

"That's not what I'm asking," Patricia said impatiently. "I want to know *what happened*." She leaned forward and wiggled her eyebrows suggestively. "You know—between you and Nick."

Rachel sighed. "For a moment, it looked like just about everything was going to happen."

"And then?" Patricia prompted.

"And then...nothing."

"Nothing?" Olivia and Patricia queried simultaneously.

"Less than nothing." Rachel shook her head. "One minute, things were starting to get intense, and the next minute, they ground to a complete halt. After that, he gave me such a wide berth that you'd think I was leaking toxic chemicals."

"He gave you the cold shoulder?"

"Not cold, exactly. More like distant. And polite." Frustration surged through Rachel's chest. "Unbelievably polite—as if I were a little old lady or something. He did everything but bow and call me ma'am. He was so darned polite, I felt like slapping him."

Patricia chortled. "Sounds like he's keeping a tight rein on himself around you."

"Well, he might be polite, but he sure doesn't see you as a little old lady," Olivia said. She grinned at Patricia. "Rachel and Nick met with Lucas and me this morning to discuss the legalities of their new audit guidelines, and Nick couldn't keep his eyes off Rachel. He was so absorbed in staring at her that Lucas had to repeat the same question three times."

Patricia wagged her eyebrows mischievously. "Sounds like you're doing something right."

Rachel grinned ruefully. "He might be staring, but he's acting so distant, he probably needs binoculars to do it."

Patricia rubbed her hands together in glee. "This is perfect! You *want* to make him uncomfortable around you."

"I do?"

"Sure. The more miserable he is, the more motivated he'll be to change."

Rachel took a sip of her soda. "Yeah, well, I hope his idea of change doesn't include a transfer to the far side of the world. He tends to seek geographic cures to romantic problems."

"But he can't," Patricia pointed out. "Not if he doesn't want to accept a demotion. Now that he's in charge of all of the corporation's accounting operations, there's no higher position to transfer to."

"That's right, Rachel," Olivia agreed. "You've got him roped in."

"Not yet, but I'm working on it." Rachel grinned. "I hope to complete the job in two weeks in St. John."

"How are the scuba lessons going?" Olivia asked.

"Great. I'm scheduled to take my open water tests this weekend."

"What's that?"

"It's where I finally go scuba diving in something besides a swimming pool. I'm going to Cancún with my class."

"Cancún?" Olivia sighed dreamily. "Wow!"

Nick walked into the room at that very moment. He paused in the doorway as he caught sight of Rachel, then proceeded in. Olivia nudged Patricia.

Nick smiled at the table of women. "Did I hear Olivia say you're going to Cancún, Patricia?" Nick asked.

"Not me. Rachel."

Nick glanced at Rachel, his eyes full of surprise. He abruptly looked away.

"Seems like I remember reading on your résumé that you once worked in Cancún," Patricia said chattily.

Nick stiffly nodded and headed to the soda machine. "I helped open the Barrington Resort there."

"Well, then, maybe you can give Rachel some pointers on what sights to see and what restaurants to try."

Rachel kicked her friend under the table, trying to get her to quit baiting him. Nick pushed his coins into the machine, then turned and looked at her, the flat line of his mouth showing clear displeasure. "I didn't know you were going to Mexico. Kind of sudden, isn't it?"

"Not really."

"Oh, I see. It's just something you deliberately chose not to mention."

The remark hung in the air, biting and personal.

"I didn't know that you'd be interested."

Nick pushed the button on the machine harder than necessary. "It's standard procedure to put in a request for vacation time two weeks in advance."

"Oh, I'm not taking any time off," Rachel said quickly. "I'll leave Friday after work and come back Sunday evening."

Olivia shot Patricia a pointed look. "Speaking of time, it's time for us to get back to work."

"But I've got five more minutes of break time left," Patricia protested, clearly reluctant to leave just when things were getting interesting.

Casting a meaningful glance at Patricia, Olivia rose. "I need to talk to you about that vacant secretarial position in the legal department." She jerked her head toward the door. "Come on. You don't want to leave a pregnant woman without adequate support staff, do you?"

"Okay, okay," Patricia mumbled, reluctantly getting to her feet.

The two women left the room, leaving Rachel alone with Nick.

"This trip is a little out of character, don't you think?" he said in a curt tone.

"I don't know what you mean."

"I mean it's unlike you, traipsing off to a place like Cancún all by yourself." The overly polite tone he'd used all week was gone, replaced by an irritated growl.

Rachel lifted her chin. "Who said I was going alone?"

A nerve flexed in Nick's jaw. "I see."

"No, you don't see." Weeks of pent-up frustration tightened Rachel's chest. Placing her hands on the table, she pushed back her chair and rose to face him. "There are a lot of things about me you don't see at all. What you think is out-of-character behavior might just be a side of me you haven't seen before. Believe it or not, I'm capable of growing and changing.'' She regarded him hotly. ''Unlike some people I know.''

''Well, I don't like the changes you've been making recently.''

''You don't even know what those changes are. What you don't like, Nick Delaney, is your reaction to what you *think* they are.'' Rachel snatched up her can of cola. ''Maybe you should ask yourself why it bothers you so much.'' Turning on her heel, she abruptly marched out of the room.

There was no use trying to talk sense into Nick, no point in trying to convince him that despite his convictions to the contrary, he was more than capable of long-term commitment—that he had, in fact, been committed to her for two years.

He had to discover it for himself. She hoped to high heavens that he'd do so on their trip to St. John. She'd do her best to push him along, but she was more than a little afraid that Nick's resistance to permanence might be the most permanent thing about him.

''You made it just in time,'' the smiling blond flight attendant said two weeks later as Nick stepped aboard the plane to St. John with Jenny in his arms. ''I was getting ready to close the door.''

''It took longer to get a baby packed and to the airport than I figured it would.'' Not to mention the time required to deal with a diaper emergency, race back to the house to retrieve a forgotten pacifier and change both their clothes after Jenny dumped a bottle of purple grape juice all over them both.

The flight attendant smiled at Jenny. ''Were you giving your daddy a hard time this morning?''

Daddy. It was funny how the word no longer bothered

him. In fact, the sound of it sent an unaccustomed burst of pride rushing through him.

The flight attendant reached forward to touch the baby's white-blond curls, causing the child to shyly bury her face against Nick's shoulder. "She's adorable," the woman said.

"Thanks." Clutching the baby in his arms, Nick maneuvered his way up the narrow aisle, trying to keep from bumping the aisle-seated passengers with the diaper bag that dangled from one shoulder and the laptop computer case that hung from the other.

"Nick—Jenny!"

Nick's pulse raced at the sound of the familiar voice, and Jenny let out a gurgle of glee.

He looked up. Sure enough, there was Rachel, sitting next to his reserved seat. His heart lurched joyfully in his chest. Dadblast it, he thought stubbornly, trying hard to squelch the reaction. He'd booked this flight just to avoid her.

"I thought you were taking the earlier flight with the rest of the corporate staff."

"I planned to, but I need to review the presentation with you, and you didn't have time to meet with me at the office. So I asked the corporate travel planner to book me on your flight so we could discuss it on the way."

Great, just great. He'd managed to avoid her for the past two weeks, but as a result, he was now stuck beside her for a four-hour flight.

He sighed and slipped the diaper bag off his shoulder. He couldn't really blame her, he thought guiltily; by avoiding her, he'd made it hard for her to do her job. All the same, he wished he could blame her for something. He wanted to find some fault that would break the spell she had on him, the spell that caused this tight, tender achiness in his chest whenever he thought about her.

And it seemed he couldn't stop thinking about her. Her,

and her blasted trip to Cancún. It had been hovering in his mind like a pesky mosquito ever since he'd learned about it.

Not that he wanted to know anything about it. He didn't. He didn't want to know what she'd done or where she'd eaten or what sights she'd seen.

Most of all, he didn't want to know who she'd gone with.

The very thought made his stomach churn. She'd returned on Monday all tanned and smiling, and he couldn't help but imagine all the things she might be smiling about. It ate at his insides like battery acid. Especially at night, when he lay in that big, draped bed, the bed where he'd held her and kissed her and could have made her his for all time.

Jenny grunted and held out her arms toward Rachel. "I'll hold her while you put away your bags," Rachel said.

Nick released the baby, then stashed his computer in the overhead bin and reluctantly settled into the seat next to Rachel. The exotic scent of her new perfume filled his nostrils, making him wonder again who she'd bought it to impress.

"Where's Mrs. Evans?" Rachel asked. "I thought she was coming with you."

Nick shoved the diaper bag under the seat in front of him. "She planned to, but an old friend died and she stayed behind to attend the funeral. She'll be joining us tomorrow."

The flight attendant at the front of the plane began her preflight spiel, and they lapsed into silence as the plane taxied to the runway.

The moment the plane was airborne, Jenny started to whimper, then burst into ear-splitting cries. Her wails were loud and desperate, and reverberated through the plane.

"Hey there, Jenny—what's the matter?" Nick asked. He reached for the child, but she turned her head and clung to

Rachel. He knew it was irrational, but the baby's rejection stung.

"It might be her ears," Rachel said.

Nick regarded the sobbing baby worriedly. "Dr. Jackson checked her last week and said her ear infection was all gone."

"The change in air pressure often bothers a baby's ears on takeoff and landing," Rachel explained. "Do you have a bottle in her bag? It'll help if we can get her to keep swallowing."

Nick retrieved the pink bag, then dug through it until he located a bottle. He pulled off the white protective cover and passed it to Rachel.

With soft murmurs, she persuaded the baby to take the bottle. After a few big gulps, Jenny burped, then gave a big, gummy grin.

Rachel smiled at Nick. "My guess is that her ears just cleared."

Relief filled Nick's chest. "Boy, am I glad you knew what to do. She sounded miserable."

"A few more minutes of crying like that, and everyone on the plane would have been in the same condition."

Nick returned Rachel's grin, a burst of warmth easing the constriction in his chest. She always seemed to know what to do. Despite the tension between them, something about her gave him a sense of comfort and he couldn't help but be glad she was here.

Jenny seemed to feel it, too. The baby was grinning up at Rachel, a look of adoration on her cherubic face. "Ma-ma."

Nick's breath froze in his throat. "Did—did she just say something?"

As if to answer, Jenny reached up a tiny hand to Rachel's face. "Ma-ma," she repeated.

"She just called you Mama," Nick said.

Rachel gazed at the baby, her face glowing. She glanced at Nick, her eyes filled with amazed joy.

Nick realized his brow was pulled in a hard frown, the corners of his mouth stretched in displeasure. He knew it was irrational, knew it wasn't Rachel's fault that the baby was so attached to her. It probably wasn't even her fault that *he* was so attached to her.

But this had to stop. It was one thing for him to play with fire, but it was quite another to expose Jenny to it. The child had recently lost her parents. She didn't need her heart broken all over again.

He knew with sudden clarity what he had to do. He had to keep Rachel out of Jenny's life. He couldn't afford to let the child grow any more emotionally attached to her.

He couldn't afford to grow any more emotionally attached to her, either. He needed to sever all personal ties with Rachel, completely, thoroughly, once and for all. It was imperative that he treat her as a co-worker and nothing more. If it proved impossible, he'd have to take drastic action.

He might as well start now. "What did you need to discuss about your presentation?" he asked curtly.

"Oh, that can wait until later. I'm sure Jenny will take a nap soon."

"If she does, I'll need to use that time to review my own notes." Nick kept his voice impersonal and businesslike. "Let's go ahead and get down to business."

Hurt. The emotion flickered across Rachel's face. He could see it in her parted lips, her furrowed brow, but most of all, in her pained blue eyes. She rapidly composed her features, but hurt continued to shadow her eyes.

"Then you'd better take Jenny so I can reach my brief-case," she said softly, handing him the child.

She knew, he thought guiltily. She knew he didn't like Jenny calling her Mama, knew he was deliberately distancing himself from her. The realization sent a surge of grief flowing through him, making the cold, empty spot in his chest grow wider.

She bent to retrieve her briefcase from under the seat, and he forced his eyes away. He didn't want to see the slender column of her spine or the way her hair spilled forward around her face or the way it parted to reveal the white, tender skin at the nape of her neck. He didn't want to remember all the things about her that prowled through his dreams at night and haunted his waking hours. He didn't want to feel all the things she stirred inside him.

It would end, sooner or later. Good things always did. And the better something was, the more you missed it when it was gone. It was better to completely end it now.

He leaned his head back against the headrest and blew out a deep sigh. He had thought he was over Rachel, had thought he could deal with working with her again, but he'd been wrong. If he couldn't control the situation, he'd have no choice but to leave again.

Leaving wouldn't be so simple now that he was a vice president, he thought grimly. Most likely he'd have to find a position with another firm.

He'd give it one last chance. From now on, he'd do his absolute best to keep his relationship with Rachel all business, strictly business and nothing but business. If he found that he couldn't, he'd have to make some serious changes. For Jenny's sake, as well as Rachel's.

Not to mention his own.

Rachel walked down the winding path from the resort's main building to the marina two days later, staring pensively at the ground. The pathway was lined with giant palms, brilliant bougainvillea, pink azaleas and other tropical plants she couldn't name, but she was too worried to appreciate the beauty of her surroundings.

She'd pinned her whole future on this trip, and things weren't going as she hoped. She hadn't managed to break

through Nick's wall of reserve at all, she thought with dis
gust. She'd only succeeded in driving him to build it talle
and thicker than ever.

Not that he was rude. She almost wished he was, becaus
then, at least, she'd be getting a reaction out of him. In
stead, he was once again being impeccably polite.

Impeccably polite and virtually invisible, she though
glumly, following the path around a bend. He pulled mor
disappearing acts than Houdini. She seldom saw him out
side of business meetings, and when she did, he made sur
he was surrounded by plenty of other people.

Instead of closing the distance between them as she'
hoped, the trip had only widened it, and she knew exactl
when it had happened: on the plane, when Jenny called he
Mama. It had terrified him.

It had terrified her, too, even though it had melted he
heart into a puddle. She would love nothing more than
actually be the child's mother, but she wasn't. And the wa
Nick was acting, chances were slim she ever would be. Sh
bit her lip, blinking back the tears that threatened her eye

Things couldn't continue as they were. Nick either ha
to make a commitment to her, or she had to stay out of th
child's life. She couldn't allow the child to get any mor
attached to her.

The scuba trip today was her last chance. To make sur
she made the most of it, she'd visited the marina yesterda
and enlisted the help of the dive boat operator, Harry, tij
ping him copiously to make sure she was paired with Nic
on the dive.

Harry waved at her now as she approached the sma
building at the end of the path. "Great day for a dive!" h
called in a lilting Caribbean accent. He hoisted a scuba tan
on his shoulder and grinned broadly, flashing large, whi
teeth. "Perfect day to go fishin', too." He winked or
brown eye. "Yessirree. Jus' the kind of day to catch
really big one."

Chuckling to himself, Harry carried the tank on board a boat tethered at the end of the dock and slipped it into a slot on a metal rack. Rachel blushed in embarrassment. She'd tried not to give away the reason she wanted to be paired with Nick, but Harry had immediately guessed that a romantic motive was behind the odd request.

"Don't worry, miss," Harry had assured her. "I'll make sure you and your young man are buddied up. I'll try to give you two some privacy underwater, too."

The quiet hum of an electric cart, the resort's standard means of transportation, sounded on the path behind her. Her heart pounding, she turned around to see Nick and four resort controllers who had attended the conference climb out as soon as it slid to a halt.

Nick froze in his tracks the moment he caught sight of her. "Rachel. What are you doing here?"

She brushed a strand of hair from her eyes, doing her best to look nonchalant. "Going on the dive."

He stared as if she'd lost her mind. "But you don't swim. You told me you're afraid of water."

"Not anymore. I'm now a certified scuba diver." She proudly reached into the mesh bag on her arm that held her flippers and dive mask, pulled out a laminated card and handed it to him.

Nick gazed at it for a long moment, then looked up, his expression puzzled. "But how? When?"

"I took lessons in Phoenix. Then I did my checkout dive a few weekends ago in Cancún."

She could practically see his guard go up. "Well, you're just a beginner. I don't know that it's a good idea for you to go on this dive."

"Oh, she'll be fine," Harry chimed in. "Garden Cay is an easy site."

"I dove it last year," chimed in the controller of Barrington's Miami resort. "We had a beginner along then and there was no problem."

"Since you're worried about her, though, Mr. Delaney, let's pair you with her," Harry suggested. "That way you can keep a close eye on her."

Damn, Nick thought darkly. The cardinal rule of diving was always to use the buddy system. There was no way he could object to Harry's suggestion without looking like a complete and total cad.

Dadblast it—and dadblast the way Rachel looked in those tight pink shorts and that low-cut tank top. It was impossible to think straight when she was standing there looking like that.

Harry waved his hand, motioning the group to gather around. "Okay, everybody—let me see your C-cards, then let's board the boat."

One by one, the divers showed Harry their certification cards, then filed aboard a small open craft sporting the name *Sea Witch*. Nick found himself seated beside Rachel on the long bench that lined the side of the boat.

"So when did you turn into Aqua Girl?" he asked.

Harry started the boat engine. Rachel moved closer to be heard over the loud roar.

"When I learned about this trip. I thought it sounded like fun."

"But what about your fear of water?"

Rachel shrugged. "Well, when I realized how much my fear was holding me back from doing things I'd really like to do, I decided it was time to conquer it."

"How did you do that?"

"It was so simple, I'm ashamed I didn't do it sooner." She brushed a strand of windblown hair away from her face. "I simply got in the shallow water of the swimming pool at my apartment and gradually worked my way deeper. Patricia and Sophia came with me for support. I started swimming in the shallow end, and before I knew what had happened, I was over my head."

Just like I was with you. The thought made Nick frown. "When did you take dive classes?"

"In the evenings."

The evenings. All the time he'd thought she was seeing someone else, she actually had been taking scuba lessons? A heavy weight deep inside lightened and lifted. "Why didn't you tell me?"

"I wanted to surprise you." Her eyes looked as blue as the water around them. "So did I?"

Had she been taking classes *all* of those nights? he wondered. And what about the trip to Cancún? She said she'd done her checkout dive there, but she could have easily arranged that through a local dive shop. Who had gone with her?

"Did I?" she asked again.

"Did you what?"

"Surprise you."

Nick nodded. "Sure did."

"I hope you don't mind my coming along today." Her brow creased as she regarded him. "I promise you won't have to worry about baby-sitting me. I had more air left in my tank after my checkout dive than anyone else in my class. My instructor said it was a sign I was relaxed in the water."

Something in her words struck a chord in Nick. Narrowing his eyes, he looked at her sharply. "Did you say you did your checkout dive with your *class?*"

Rachel nodded. "The trip to Cancún was part of the course."

Relief poured through him like water down a rain spout. "So you went with a group of people, not one specific person?"

A hint of amusement gleamed in Rachel's eyes. "There were five of us. I promise I was well chaperoned at all times."

Nick was glad that Harry chose that moment to switch

off the boat engine so he didn't have to come up with a response. "It, uh, looks like we've arrived. Time to suit up."

Harry lowered an anchor, then turned toward the tanks, which were fitted in a rack and fastened to vestlike apparatuses called buoyancy compensators, commonly known as BCs. "I've got everyone's gear all set except for yours, Mr. Delaney. You said you'd be bringing your own equipment."

"That's right. All I need is a tank."

"Help yourself," Harry said.

Nick ambled over, hoisted one on his shoulder, then carried it back to his seat beside Rachel. Digging into the large bag he'd stowed under the seat, he fastened his regulator to the valve, then turned the knob on the top of the tank, listening for the telltale swoosh of air. He picked up the mouthpiece and took a breath to check it. Satisfied, he fastened the tank onto his BC, then peeled off his shirt.

He turned to see Rachel staring at him. "Do you need some help?"

"N-no," she said, averting her eyes.

She waited until he was occupied adjusting his weight belt before she peeled off her shorts and tank top. When he looked up, the breath caught in his throat. Good grief; she was wearing a black swimsuit edged in neon colors. It was cut low on the top and high on the leg, and it made him feel as if his eyes were bugging a mile out of his head.

The fear of water wasn't the only thing Rachel was overcoming, Nick thought ruefully. The way she looked in that swimsuit, she was rapidly overcoming every shred of his resistance to her.

She pulled on her flippers, then Harry helped her into her BC as Nick slipped on his own. Once everyone had donned all their gear and was seated on the side of the boat, Harry stood up.

"Okay, everyone. Let's go over the hand signals." Harry

held out his hand, fist closed, and pointed his thumb up. "What does this mean?"

Rachel smiled. "That's easy. 'Let's go up.' And if you turn it the other way, it means 'Let's go down.'"

Harry beamed approvingly. "What's this one?" Harry placed his hand at his neck, his fingers straight and horizontal.

"That means 'out of air,'" the Miami controller contributed.

"Very good." Harry curved his fingers and held them to his mouth.

"That means to share your air supply by passing the regulator back and forth," said the controller from Houston.

"It's called 'buddy breathing,'" Rachel piped up.

"That's right," Harry said. He held his hand out and made a fist.

"That means danger," one of the other controllers called.

"One more. What does this mean?" He made a circle with his thumb and forefinger.

"That's easy," Rachel said. "'Everything's okay.'"

Harry smiled broadly. "You guys know your stuff. One more thing before we go in—I expect all of you to follow Harry's three rules of diving."

He held up a finger. "Rule number one—never panic. Any situation is manageable if you keep your head. Rule number two—never hold your breath as you ascend. Your lungs could burst as the air expands. And rule number three—always stay close to your buddy." Harry looked around. "Any questions? No? Well, then I guess we're all set."

Nick looked at Rachel, expecting to see fear or at least a little nervousness, but her eyes registered only excitement as she fitted her mask on her face. He had to admit she looked like she knew what she was doing. She inflated her BC, took an experimental breath of air from the mouthpiece and checked her pressure gauge one last time. Placing one hand protectively over her mask, she gave a jaunty thumbs-up, then fell backward out of the boat in perfect form.

As soon as he saw her safely bobbing on the surface, Nick followed her into the water. He was immediately submerged in sensation—the coolness of the water, the loud roar of his own breathing through the regulator, the salty taste of the ocean. He spotted Rachel and reached her side in two strokes of his flippers, then questioningly flashed her the "okay" signal. Her eyes smiling, she returned it, then hit the air release button on her BC so she could descend. Taking her free hand, Nick did the same.

He looked down. The water was so clear that it gave him a brief dizzying sensation. It was like looking through air, like hovering off the roof of a six-story building.

Rachel tightened her grip on his hand and excitedly pointed down to the mountains of coral below them. A moment later, she pointed to a school of blue and yellow Queen Angelfish drifting by, their wide bodies shaped like the spades on a deck of cards. He was still watching the angelfish when Rachel tugged on his hand to point out a shimmering wall of silverfish, swimming in such an enormous school that they looked like a giant metallic shield.

When Rachel yanked at his hand yet again to point out a floating jellyfish, Nick grinned despite the regulator clenched in his teeth. He'd been on a lot of previous dives, and most of them were technically a lot more challenging than this one. He'd been on deeper dives, dives into caves, and dives in water so murky, he could hardly see his own hand, but none of them had given him the thrill he was feeling right now with Rachel.

She looked at Nick, her eyes filled with childlike wonder, and pointed up. Nick followed her gaze, and felt his chest expand with an unexpected sense of wonder, too. Waves made cloudlike patterns on the liquid sky. Fish drifted through the current like birds through the air.

Rachel squeezed his hand as they neared the bottom, saying as much with that touch as anyone had ever said to him aloud. They were in another world together, a private world that excluded everything but the here and now.

Come to think of it, it was a world a lot like the world they shared when they kissed.

Deliberately trying to force his thoughts to safer territory, he looked down. They were near the coral now, hovering just above it. A brilliant-hued parrotfish, as brightly colored as its feathered namesake, munched at a spindly stem of finger coral. Lacy sea fans in green and purple waved atop staghorn and brain coral. Banded butterfly fish, looking for all the world like fat little zebras, darted among it. An enormous lone grouper, bumpy and brown, approached them, apparently curious about the interlopers on its turf.

They floated around, exploring the reef, pointing out discoveries to each other with delight. Nick felt his heart flood with a sense of peace and an unfamiliar feeling he could only call joy.

And then, suddenly, something was wrong. Terribly wrong. He inhaled, but he couldn't draw air.

He adjusted the regulator in his mouth and tried again, only to inhale into an airless vacuum.

Good Lord. He was sixty-five feet below the surface, buddied with an amateur diver, and he was out of air. He started to gesture to Rachel that he needed to buddy breathe, then hesitated. He didn't want her to panic and create a situation where she, too, was in trouble.

She gazed at him, her brow furrowed. He desperately looked around for the other divers. The closest pair of divers was thirty yards or more away, and they were heading the opposite direction.

Damn. He might pass out before he reached them. His chest was already burning with the need for oxygen.

He glanced back at Rachel. Something in his expression must have signaled his distress, because the next thing he knew, she'd pulled the regulator from her mouth and was holding it out to him.

He looked into her eyes. Her gaze was trusting and calm, and she nodded encouragingly. Placing the mouthpiece between his lips, he blew into it to clear it, then inhaled a sweet lungful of air. He rapidly drew another breath, then passed it back to Rachel. She took a breath and handed it back.

Arms entwined around each other, they began a slow ascent to the surface, sharing a single source of air. It was intimacy of the highest order, more intimate than making love.

Maybe it *was* love—love as a verb.

The thought jarred him, but not as much as it would have under other circumstances. Life had taken on a surreal aspect, as if time had slowed and nearly stopped. He was filled with an eerie sense of well-being, a feeling that made no sense under the circumstances.

It made no sense, yet it was.

Rachel was. And he'd never been closer, never been more profoundly connected to another human being in his life. He was so focused on her and on this moment that he was surprised when his face emerged from the water.

Air. Everywhere. Nick gulped hungrily at it. So much fresh air. Such a wonderful abundance of the sweet, breathable stuff.

Drinking it in, he guided Rachel to the boat and steered her to the back, grabbing hold of the ladder that extended into the water from a wooden platform. "I'll go first so I can pull you up. Hold on tight for one minute."

Nick scaled the ladder, dropped his BC and tank in one smooth motion, then turned back to Rachel. "Can you find the bottom rung with your foot?"

Rachel groped at the ladder, then gave a weak nod. Now that she and Nick were safely at the surface, her muscles seemed as rubbery as her air hose. Her strength had vanished, leaving her drained and exhausted.

"I'm going to reach down and lift the top of your tank so you won't have to bear the weight of your gear as you climb up. Ready?"

Rachel gave another trembling nod and fit a flippered foot onto the rung.

Three more steps, and she was in the boat.

Two more steps, and Nick had unfastened her dive gear.

One more step, and she was in his arms.

Chapter Ten

Sensation after sensation washed over Rachel as Nick pulled her against him—the solid hardness of his chest, the ocean scent of his skin, the welcome warmth of his arms around her. For a long minute he simply held her, a minute in which the sound of the waves and the beat of their hearts more than filled the silence.

"Are you all right?" he finally asked, pulling back far enough to look down at her.

Numbly Rachel nodded.

"You're shivering. Are you cold?"

"No. I think this is the aftermath of being scared."

Nick ran his hands down her arms. "I never would have known you were frightened. You looked so calm." He held her at arm's length and gazed at her, the corners of his eyes crinkling as he grinned. "You were amazing. Especially for a beginner diver. You saved my life—do you realize that?"

She mustered a wobbly grin. "What happened down there?"

"My regulator must have broken. The gauge read that

there was still plenty of air in the tank, but all of a sudden I couldn't breathe.''

"Why didn't you signal me that you were out of air?''

Nick hesitated. "You're a brand-new diver, and you'd just gotten over your fear of deep water. I didn't want to scare you. I was hoping to get the attention of one of the other divers.''

"But I didn't know what was going on. I thought maybe you'd been stung by a ray or a man-of-war or something.'' Rachel's gaze scanned his face. "I was scared, all right, but only because I didn't know what was happening to you.''

He rubbed his hands up and down her upper arms, his eyes warm and earnest. "I'm sorry. I just didn't want to put you in any danger.''

Despair and frustration crashed over her. How had she managed to achieve the opposite of what she'd set out to do?

"But, Nick—that's what the buddy system is all about. Two people helping each other, being there for each other in case either one gets in trouble.'' Hot tears formed in her eyes. "The last thing I wanted to be was a burden. I took up diving because I wanted to show you I could be an equal partner.''

Nick's brow wrinkled in confusion. "I don't understand. I've always seen you that way.''

Frustrated tears coursed down her cheeks. "I wanted you to see that I won't hold you back. That I'm not always b-b-boring.''

"Boring?" Nick stared at her, his eyes wide and incredulous. "You thought I believed you were *boring?*''

Rachel nodded miserably.

"Good Lord, Rachel, how could you think a thing like that?'' He stepped closer, his hand moving to her back. "Don't you know you're the most exciting woman I've ever known?''

His gaze poured down on her like warm syrup. "Don't you know how you make me feel? When I'm around you, I find it hard to think straight. I had an awful time during the conference. Every time I'd look across the room and see you, my heart would start pounding and my thoughts would stray and I'd nearly forget what I was saying. When I looked at you, the last thing on my mind was audit procedures."

Rachel's heart fluttered furiously. "What was the first thing?" she whispered.

"Doing this."

His fingers tightened on her back, drawing her to him. But this time the embrace wasn't warm and comforting. This time it was hot and needy, and when he claimed her lips, the kiss was wild and hungry. His mouth ravished hers, and then, at length, it gentled and slowed. He took her bottom lip tenderly between his own, drawing on the sensitive flesh until Rachel moaned aloud. His hands slid to the sides of her breasts as his lips moved to her ear. Shivers chased through her at the delicious warmth of his breath, the slow, exquisite slide of his fingers.

The boat rocked on the waves, and Rachel's world rocked with it. Everything in the universe seemed to coalesce into the warmth of his body, the touch of his hands, the demanding heat of his lips. The thin, wet fabric of her swimsuit left her feeling naked against him. She molded herself against him, feeling the hard heat of his desire and the answering liquid flame deep within her.

She felt as though she'd been born for this moment, as though everything in her life had been a prelude to this very second. The words welled up and simply wouldn't stay inside. "I love you," she whispered.

She ached to hear him say it back. She needed to hear it, needed it like oxygen. Her heart sent a desperate prayer winging heavenward.

Nick went very still. His hands dropped to his side, then

he stepped away. His eyes grew shuttered and dark, his posture rigid.

And his silence was very loud, telling her all that he did not say.

Her life seemed to crash and burn around her, sending her dreams up in smoke, turning her fondest hopes to ashes. She heard a metallic clink at the rear of the boat. For a moment it didn't register. Her pain was so intense that for all she knew, it could have been the sound of her heart shattering into a thousand pieces.

"The other divers are back." Nick reached out and squeezed her hand. "We'll talk more later."

Rachel watched him stride toward the back of the boat, knowing there would be no later. There was no reason for it. His silence had said it all.

He was unwilling or unable to love her in return. Discussing it further would serve no purpose. There was no point in trying to hang on to something that simply wasn't there.

There was no point in staying on at the resort an extra day, either, for the next day's dive. She'd pack up her shredded heart, her tattered pride and her broken dreams, and she'd take the next flight home.

Nick stared out his office window at the Barrington parking lot on Monday morning, his eyes zeroing in on the blue Toyota in the back row.

Rachel's car. She was here, somewhere in the building.

He gazed down at the report he was trying to read, but the columns of numbers marched meaninglessly across the page as his thoughts kept drifting back to Rachel.

He hadn't been able to get his mind off her ever since this weekend. She'd been extremely quiet on the boat ride back to shore after the dive trip. He knew he hadn't handled things well, but her declaration of love had made him feel as if he were running out of air all over again.

He didn't want her to love him. He didn't want to love her. Love implied permanence, commitment, marriage. Marriage meant a loss of freedom, a slow and gradual decline into a life of stifling routine. He'd had a life of routine before, and he knew he didn't want it. He wanted to live outside the box, to color outside the lines, to be free to grow and change as he saw fit without having to answer to anyone.

With a sigh of frustration, Nick turned his attention back to the piece of paper on his desk, only to be interrupted by a faint tapping on his partially open office door.

He looked up, and his pulse rate accelerated. "Rachel. Come in."

He rose and rounded his desk as she entered the room. She'd never looked lovelier. Her bright coral suit set off her tan, and her legs looked longer than ever in flesh-colored high heels.

Nick motioned to one of the two flame-stitched chairs before his desk.

Rachel shook her head. "What I have to say won't take long."

Trepidation knotted Nick's stomach. Trying hard to appear calmer than he felt, he settled himself on the edge of his desk.

Rachel handed him a piece of paper.

"What's this?"

"A request for a transfer to Barrington's San Diego resort. The chief controller told me at the conference that he was looking for an assistant controller and asked if I'd be interested. I told him I wasn't, but after..." Her voice broke. She cleared her throat and lifted her chin. "After I thought it over, I decided I am. I've already checked with Personnel. Patricia says that if you recommend me, Rex will approve the transfer."

A jolt of pain stabbed through his heart. He should have been expecting something like this, but it caught him off guard. He rose and took a step toward her, pulling his eyebrows into a frown. "Rachel, I don't want to run you off."

She held herself rigidly, her arms at her side. "I can't stay here, Nick. I can't work for you anymore." Her head tilted a fraction of an inch higher. "Besides, I've decided to go back to college and earn a degree in early-childhood education. In a few years, I'd like to open my own preschool. The assistant controller's position will require fewer late nights and less travel, so it'll be easier for me to go to school."

An old, familiar heaviness filled Nick's chest—the same aching emptiness he'd experienced at eighteen when his father had thrown him out of the house. "So you're going to follow your dreams."

"The one that's within my reach."

He ached to soothe that anguished look from her eyes, to pull her into his arms and hold her and tell her everything would be all right.

But he couldn't. He knew she'd never believe him. He didn't believe it himself.

He blew out a deep breath and gazed at her, feeling as forlorn and lonely as he'd ever felt in his life. "You know I won't stand in your way. If you're sure it's what you want, I'll write the letter."

Rachel nodded stiffly. "There's one more thing. I have several weeks of unused vacation time. I'd like to use two of them between now and when I start my new job."

"Sure. When did you want your leave to begin?"

"Immediately."

She sure wasn't wasting any time. But then, he thought ruefully, he couldn't fault her on that score. He'd left just as abruptly two years ago.

He swallowed, his throat tight and dry. "Okay. If that's what you want."

"It is." She turned to go. "Well, I'll go clear out my office."

Nick reached out and grabbed her arm. "Rachel..."

She looked up and met his gaze. He stared at her, searching for something to say. There was nothing left to discuss, but he needed to somehow delay her departure just one moment more.

"I'll miss you," he finally managed.

Her lips quivered as they haltingly curved into a sad smile. Her eyes grew full and overbright. Without a word, she turned and walked out the door.

Amazing how empty a room full of furniture could look, Nick thought the next day as he strode past Rachel's office on his way to lunch. The desktop was naked, the corners of the room were bare of the plants Rachel so carefully tended and the shelves were stripped of photos and personal effects. Without Rachel, the room seemed cold and barren.

Which was pretty much the way he felt inside. He turned and headed resolutely down the hall. He was going to have to stop taking this route to and from his office, he thought grimly. He'd fallen into the habit of routinely passing by Rachel's office door not because it was the fastest route to his office, but because he'd hoped to catch a glimpse of her.

He'd built a surprising number of habits around Rachel, he thought, jabbing the button at the elevator bank. He'd started visiting the break room at ten-thirty in the morning because that was when she usually took a break with her friends, and he frequently did the same thing at three in the afternoon. This morning when he'd stepped into the room, Patricia, Sophia, Molly, Olivia and Cindy had eyed him with such reproach that he'd hastily grabbed a cola and headed back to his office, vowing to change his routine.

He wanted to avoid Rachel's buddies at lunch, too. Well, at least he wouldn't have to worry about it today, he thought, stepping into the elevator. Instead of going to any of the local restaurants where he was likely to encounter them, he planned to take his scuba regulator to his favorite dive shop and have it repaired. And while he was there, he was going to ask about upcoming dive expeditions. Planning a fresh adventure was his standard cure for the blues.

Maybe he'd explore an underwater cave or a shipwreck site. Or maybe he'd combine a dive trip with something even more exciting, like skydiving or speed boat racing. The more depressed he felt, the larger an adventure he usually planned.

It was odd, but nothing sounded very appealing this time. The elevator doors slid open and he stepped out into the lobby. Perhaps it was because of Jenny, he mused. Maybe having the responsibility of a child to raise had dampened his enthusiasm for danger.

That was probably part of it, he silently acknowledged, pushing through the lobby door and stepping into the bright sunshine of the parking lot, but that wasn't all. The truth was, Rachel's departure had dampened his enthusiasm for everything.

Nothing sounded fun or exciting anymore. Without Rachel, life seemed as flat and empty as the most barren stretch of the Arizona desert.

Unlocking his car door, he climbed in, started the engine and drove to the dive shop. Ten minutes later, he pulled into the parking lot of a small stucco building with a large red and white dive flag flapping by the door.

He killed the engine and picked up his regulator from the passenger seat. Turning it over in his hand, he examined it closely. The depth gauge, the pressure gauge, the tubing, the mouthpiece—everything looked okay. Nothing in its appearance gave away the fact it was broken inside.

Just like him.

His stomach tightening, he stared at the regulator. It was just a bunch of metal and rubber, yet he trusted it with his life. It had let him down once, but here he was, ready to get it fixed and give it another chance.

Rachel had never let him down. She'd always been there when he needed her. Hell, she'd even saved his life, yet he wasn't willing to give her a chance at all.

He studied the round metal gauges and the long black tubes, his mind spinning. When he was dozens of feet underwater, he was completely dependent on this ugly appliance to stay alive. He was tied to the thing, yet it didn't limit his freedom.

It expanded it. When he relied on this regulator and a tank of air, he was able to explore a world he would otherwise never know existed.

Maybe marriage could be like that, he thought suddenly. Maybe there was a whole other dimension to married life that he just hadn't seen. He'd never seen the underwater world until he took up scuba diving, but that hadn't made it any less real.

His heart rate accelerated. Maybe he'd been looking at this marriage thing all wrong. Instead of looking at what it could offer, he'd only been looking at what it could take.

He'd thought marriage meant losing his freedom, but what the heck *was* freedom, anyway? It was just the ability to do what he wanted.

Well, what he wanted was to be with Rachel.

Now, and for the rest of his days. He wanted to spend his life with her. With her and Jenny, and maybe another baby or two.

A feeling of freedom flowed over him, a freedom he'd never known. He loved her. He'd tried to deny it, but it was an undeniable fact. He loved her, and he wanted to marry her.

He needed to let her know. A feeling of urgency swept over him. It might not be easy to get her to hear him out. He'd hurt her twice, and she wouldn't be eager to give him another chance.

Nick gazed at the regulator, thinking hard, then suddenly snapped his fingers. "That's it!" he murmured.

With a wide grin, he set down the equipment, picked up his car phone and dialed his office.

"I don't know why I had to come back to the office for an exit interview," Rachel complained to Patricia in the Barrington elevator the next day. "I'm transferring, not leaving the company."

"It's a new company policy. Every time an employee transfers, Rex wants to get feedback on ways we can improve our systems and policies."

Rachel sighed. "Well, I don't seen why we couldn't have handled this over the phone."

Patricia lifted her shoulders. "All I know is what I'm told. The order came from Rex's office."

Rachel looked up in alarm as the elevator sailed past the third floor where the personnel offices were located. "Hey, we just passed your floor!"

Patricia smiled in what Rachel thought was an oddly sheepish manner. "My office is, uh, being used for a training session today. Since your old office is vacant, I thought we'd go there."

"Oh, no," Rachel moaned. Anywhere but the accounting department. "I don't want to have to see Nick again. I don't think I could bear it."

"It's taken care of," Patricia said soothingly. "You don't have anything to worry about."

Rachel shot her friend an uneasy glance. "You mean he's in a meeting?"

"Uh—yeah, that's right." A strange expression flitted over Patricia's face, an expression that almost looked like a grin.

Patricia was acting very weirdly today. She seemed too chipper about this whole thing. Rachel eyed her suspiciously as the elevator door opened. "This isn't some sort of surprise party setup, is it? Because I told you I don't want a going-away party. I can't deal with it under the circumstances.''

''Would you just relax? I promise this isn't a party.''

They walked down the hall to the accounting department reception area. Inside the glass double doors, Rachel froze. A large crowd was gathered outside her office—all of the accounting staff, as well as Sophia, Olivia, Cindy and Molly. Rachel looked around in dismay. Rex, Rex's assistant, Mildred, and Mike the mailman were among those smiling and greeting her.

Rachel's face flamed. ''I thought you said this wasn't a party,'' she whispered hotly to Patricia.

''It's not.''

''Well, then, what's going on? Why is everybody standing outside my old office?''

''Go on in and see.''

The crowd parted, making a path for Rachel. She tried to return her co-workers' smiles, but her heart was heavy. She was no doubt about to find her office decorated with streamers and a large Good Luck banner. She was going to kill Patricia and her other friends the moment she got them alone.

She hesitated outside the doorway.

''Go on,'' Patricia urged, giving her a nudge.

Rachel drew a deep breath and walked in, then stopped short. ''Wh-what's all this?''

She could barely believe her eyes. The room was packed with aquariums. Tank after tank lined the walls, each one filled with a dazzling display of tropical fish. Butterfly fish, angelfish, silversides and reef fish, fish of all sizes and shapes and colors, swam gracefully in clear blue water.

Even more amazing than the aquariums, however, was the inflated rubber boat sitting in the middle of the room. For inside the boat, wearing a tiny black wet suit and chewing on a snorkel, was Jenny.

Dumbfounded, Rachel turned back to the faces in the doorway. "What's going on?"

"I'll tell you what's going on." Nick stepped through the doorway, nonplussing Rachel all the more. A bright orange BC was fastened over his starched white shirt, a scuba mask dangled from around his neck and a pair of large green flippers flapped from his leather loafers. He looked ridiculous, but Rachel was too stunned to be amused.

"You and I had a conversation we needed to finish," Nick said. "So I thought I'd try to re-create the right atmosphere."

Rachel stepped back until her thighs hit the desk. She reached behind her and gripped the edge with her fingers, desperately needing to hang on to something solid. "What are you talking about?"

Nick turned to the crowd outside the door. "Excuse me, folks, but this part's private." He firmly pulled the door closed, sealing Rachel inside the room with him and Jenny.

Turning back around, he awkwardly flapped across the room toward Rachel. Jenny let out a loud gurgle of laughter. Under other circumstances, Rachel might have laughed, too, but her insides were quaking too hard.

"As I recall, you and I were on a boat in the middle of the Caribbean. You had just saved my life, then you told me you loved me."

Rachel felt her face flush scarlet. Oh, dear heavens. Surely he hadn't brought her back to the office to humiliate her.

Nick stepped closer. "I've got to tell you, sweetheart, you scared me to death. Running out of air sixty-five feet under the sea was nothing compared to what I felt when you said those three little words. And do you know why it scared me?" Nick picked up her hands and folded his fingers around hers, then his eyes claimed her gaze just as firmly.

Wordlessly, Rachel shook her head no.

"Because I love you, too. I loved you two years ago, and I love you today."

Rachel's heart felt as if it were about to bound out of her chest. She wanted to pinch herself to see if she were dreaming.

"I didn't want to love you," he continued. "I didn't want to love anybody. I was sure that love always ended in disappointment and hurt, with two people tying each other in knots and killing each other's fondest dreams. And then I got to thinking about all my goals and dreams, and I realized I'd achieved nearly all of them. All except the one I want the most, the one I think I've always wanted on such a gut-deep level I couldn't even bring myself to admit it."

"What is it?" Rachel breathed.

"A family. The kind that sticks together and plays together and supports each other and wants the best for each other. I longed for it when I was a kid, and I guess I never outgrew it." Nick inched even closer. "So I got to thinking. If you could find the courage to get back in the water and face your deepest fear, maybe I should try to do the same. I've tried to fill up the emptiness inside me with outside activities. I've climbed tall cliffs, kayaked raging rivers, parachuted out of airplanes, but unlike you, I never faced my deepest fear. I never risked my heart."

Nick squeezed her fingers tightly. "I thought if I just didn't admit how I felt about you, it would run its course and go away. But it didn't. My feelings for you just grew stronger. So I got to wondering. If this feeling won't go away when I try so hard to get rid of it, what's it likely to do if I nurture it?"

Rachel felt as if her heart would burst. Her throat felt so full of emotion that she could barely find her voice. "What are you saying?"

"I'm saying I finally figured out that life is a lot like

scuba diving. It's a whole lot better when you use the buddy system." He unzipped a pocket on his BC and handed her out a small, flat box. "I've got something for you."

With trembling hands, Rachel lifted the lid. Inside, nestled on a bed of pink tissue paper, sat a pair of lime green scuba gloves. And on the ring finger of the left hand, sparkling like the Caribbean sun, was a large diamond solitaire.

She turned to Nick, her heart in her throat. "Oh, Nick…"

He smiled, his eyes as bright as the gleaming stone. "If we're going to take the plunge, I want you to have the right equipment."

He abruptly dropped to one knee and took her hand. "I love you, Rachel. I want you to be my buddy and partner—now and forever, for wetter or dryer, on land or under the sea." His voice was husky with emotion. "Rachel, will you marry me?"

"Oh, Nick…" The look on her face must have given him his answer, for the next thing she knew, he was back on his feet and she was in his arms, kissing him with all of her heart and soul.

A long moment later, a babyish sound filtered through her fog of pleasure.

"Ma-ma. Da-da."

"She just called you Daddy!" Rachel gasped.

Nick pulled back and smiled. "See there? Even Jenny agrees that we belong together." Crossing the room, Nick stepped into the boat, picked the child up and gave her a big hug. He suddenly froze, an expression of alarm on his face.

"Uh-oh."

"Uh-oh what?"

"Jenny's struck again."

"What do you mean?"

Nick gingerly set the baby back in the boat. Straightening, he grinned and pointed to a large, wet stain on his BC. "I just discovered why they call that thing she's wearing a wet suit."

Rachel met Nick's eyes, and together they shared a heart-felt laugh—one of many that promised to fill the days ahead with joy.

* * * * *

Don't miss Patricia's story,

THE MARRIAGE MERGER,
by Vivian Leiber,

next month's LOVING THE BOSS *title, available only in Silhouette Romance.*

Silhouette Romance proudly presents an all-new, original series...

Six friends dream of marrying their bosses in this delightful new series

Come see how each month, office romances lead to happily-ever-after for six friends.

In January 1999—
THE BOSS AND THE BEAUTY by Donna Clayton

In February 1999—
THE NIGHT BEFORE BABY by Karen Rose Smith

In March 1999—
HUSBAND FROM 9 to 5 by Susan Meier

In April 1999—
THE EXECUTIVE'S BABY by Robin Wells

In May 1999—
THE MARRIAGE MERGER by Vivian Leiber

In June 1999—
I MARRIED THE BOSS by Laura Anthony

Only from

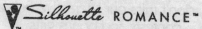

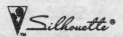

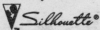

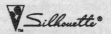

COMING NEXT MONTH